P9-EMC-837

Rocket and James
Are
Locked In!

Like us on facebook at Rocket and James
rocketandjames@gmail.com

Rocket and James Are Locked In!

Christine Albert

ARCHWAY
PUBLISHING

Copyright © 2015 Christine Albert.

Cover by Julia Kelsey.
Inside art by Paul Bertrand and Gracie Wallace.

All rights reserved. No part of this book may be used or reproduced by
any means, graphic, electronic, or mechanical, including photocopying,
recording, taping or by any information storage retrieval system
without the written permission of the author except in the case of
brief quotations embodied in critical articles and reviews.

Archway Publishing books may be ordered through booksellers or by contacting:

Archway Publishing
1663 Liberty Drive
Bloomington, IN 47403
www.archwaypublishing.com
1 (888) 242-5904

Because of the dynamic nature of the Internet, any web addresses or
links contained in this book may have changed since publication and
may no longer be valid. The views expressed in this work are solely those
of the author and do not necessarily reflect the views of the publisher,
and the publisher hereby disclaims any responsibility for them.

Any people depicted in stock imagery provided by Thinkstock are models,
and such images are being used for illustrative purposes only.
Certain stock imagery © Thinkstock.

ISBN: 978-1-4808-2293-1 (sc)
ISBN: 978-1-4808-2294-8 (e)

Library of Congress Control Number: 2015916427

Print information available on the last page.

Archway Publishing rev. date: 10/6/2015

Dedication

For Sydney and Gracie

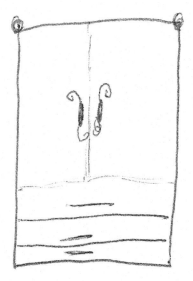

Acknowledgments

Thank you to Julia Kelsey, Paul Bertrand and Gracie Wallace for their artwork. Sydney Wallace for her creative work and ideas. A huge thank you to Denis O'Neil for editing for me.

Special thanks to my R&D supporters: Gracie Wallace, Sydney Wallace, Joe Livingston, Ann Bertrand, Ethan Crawford, Cindy Rich and Emerson Giella

And, of course, Whisper, Roscoe and Hailey. I know we missed a few walks while I was busy doing this.

Chapter 1

Circus Freaks and the Bird

My name is David, or "Rocket" to my friends. I am in the seventh grade at Grover Regional Middle and Elementary School and this is my story. Well, mine and James' story, as told by me and James. I swear everything you are about to read is true. At least that's how we see it.

Right from the start, the day had a *feel* to it. Just like Sundays *feel* like Sundays and Mondays *feel* like Mondays, this day just had a feel to it, though I'm not sure what it was. It could have been that it was the Friday before our spring break at Grover Regional Middle and Elementary School, or maybe it was the first day it actually felt like spring. Winter had finally broken and a warm front brought temperatures soaring up, well, up for our area of the world. Sometimes living here felt like what I would imagine living at the North Pole would feel like, but not today, today the temperature was expected to reach the 50's. Whatever it was, the day had a feel.

There was nothing unusual about my morning. I showered and dressed and grabbed breakfast to eat on the way as usual, shoved my stuff for school in my backpack and headed out to the bus stop. Mom and her husband (her fourth, by the way) had both already left for the day, off to do whatever it is they do during the day.

I was working on scarfing down some sort of breakfast bar as I skateboarded toward the bus, which was already there waiting for me.

Mr. Keiser, the bus driver had his usual scowl on as he watched me rolling up the street toward the open bus door. I don't get why after all this time, he still gives me that look. Here it is, April, he's had to wait for me every day since school started, he should be used to it by now. What he *should* do is start his bus route five minutes later, then we'd both be happy.

At the bus, I popped up my board, grabbed it in my non-breakfast bar hand and climbed into the bus.

"S'up Mr. K?" I jutted my chin to greet the driver. He grumbled his usual grumble and I found my seat.

Normal. Just like always, but today had that *feel*. James was already on the bus, but I don't ever sit with her. We have been in the same class since kindergarten and I guess she's OK. I still remember the first day of kindergarten when Mrs. Sally was taking attendance.

"James Whittimore?" No one answered, so she said the name again. "James Whittimore?"

A little brown haired girl in the back asked with barely a whisper, "Do you mean Jamie?"

"Well, I guess maybe I do!" Mrs. Sally answered back trying to recover from the mistake while not embarrassing Jamie too. "Maybe I should put on my reading glasses after all, huh Jamie? I'm sorry, you're absolutely right, it does say Jamie on my list."

So I made sure from that moment on, to call her James. She hated it in kindergarten and first grade, tolerated it in second and ignored me in third. Now that we are in seventh grade together, I think she has gotten used to it.

She lived two houses down from me when we lived on the tree streets, the section of town where all the streets are named after trees. We lived in number 97, she was in 101; but that was when Mom was married to Dennis (husband #2), we have moved a few times since then. Now we live by the park and we live with Mark. I teased Mom relentlessly about that when she and Mark found the apartment.

"We're seriously going to live with Mark, by the park?" and I'd make sure to drag out the 'ar' sound. "Maaarrrrk by the paaarrrk."

It's an OK place and only about a five minute board ride to James's house, but she usually meets me in the middle. James taught me how to ride, but thankfully she has a horrible memory and I've convinced her that I rode first. I think she believes me.

James's mom sells real estate in our town and her father wears a suit to work, I have no idea what he does. I only know her mom sells real estate because she helped my mom find our last three apartments.

My mom has never had a real job, she buys abandon storage lockers and sells what she finds in them, or sometimes she keeps the stuff. I wish she would just sell it all. There is seriously no reason to have 15 clocks in our apartment and about a hundred more in boxes stuffed behind the couch. Most of the clocks don't even work. So, because she has no actual job to list on apartment applications, James's mom helps her by telling the landlords that she is OK.

I don't think any of her husbands have had jobs either, at least none of them have worn suits. Each one has had some get rich quick scam that Mom falls for until she realizes that her storage locker "business" is what's paying all the bills, or some of them anyway. Mark's plan to get rich is with cell phones. He buys peoples old unwanted phones and cleans them with Windex. Then he tries to sell them on the internet. Besides clocks, I think our apartment has more phones than anywhere in the world. Clocks and Phones. Whatever.

My bus stop is the last one on the route to school, so the ride only takes 10 minutes. I wish it were longer. It would be a great place to finish my homework that's due today. We arrive at school and everyone pours into homeroom. Ms. Bethany, our teacher tries to get control but today has a feel and I think everyone can feel it. We are loud, loud, loud and nobody is sitting down, oddly enough, it doesn't seem like she cares much. She motions for us to sit in our seats, but no one is looking at her.

The principal comes on over the loud speaker for our morning announcements. This gets our attention and we start to calm down and take our seats. He goes through his usual morning news, lunch for the day, someone is having a birthday, blah, blah, blah. Then, he announces that he has a surprise for us. Terrific. A surprise from the principal, what oh what could it be? I know I'm on the edge of my seat. I roll my eyes at his announcement.

At the end of the day, he announces, there will be an assembly in the gym, he repeats that it is in the gym, not the auditorium, nope, its in the gym. We get it. Apparently, he has been in contact with the manager of some little circus that is performing over our vacation in the city and they are coming to perform for us this afternoon. It is obvious from his tone that our principal is very proud of this accomplishment of his.

I am overjoyed.

Not because I have a thing for crappy little circuses that pass through the town but because I won't have to go to math and now I won't have to finish my homework. The day is looking up already! He finishes his announcements like he always does with some little cliche he read in a book or saw on TV or something. He is certainly not clever enough to make them up himself, but he likes to take credit for them anyway. Today he says, "You are the only person responsible for your future. Make it a great day by making smart decisions".

We hear him trying to click off the loud speaker, same as

always, he needs his secretary to help him find the button. We hear this every morning.

Our principal does not exactly instill confidence.

One morning when the secretary was out sick, he left the speaker on for over an hour, we all heard everything, *everything* that happened in his office. I won't go into detail, but let me tell you now, that, funny as it was, it is not something you ever want to hear. It's amazing what people say and do when they think they are totally alone.

For whatever reason, when the announcements are being given, everyone faces the big screen on the wall where the sound comes out of. It's like we think we can hear better if we are looking that way, or maybe we are trying to be respectful of our principal by giving our undivided attention, but I doubt it. So when he is finished, and his secretary has shut off the speaker for him, we all swing around in our seats and face Ms. Bethany. Today was no different. We turned and settled in for our first lesson of the day.

Our first class is reading. We are reading *Where the Tall Grass Grows,* its a book about some farmer trying to change some farming law that the government has placed on people who grow wheat, or corn, or something. I'm not sure, it's not my favorite book.

Today Ms. Bethany wants to discuss the underlying feelings of the farmer when he realizes that he has to live by this new law. *Really? We are discussing feelings? Okay,* I slump down in my chair and listen.

The farmer in our story is called Cletus, but Ms. Bethany keeps calling him Frank. *What?* I may not have been paying complete attention to the book, but I do know the difference between Cletus and Frank. She corrects herself. Then, she does it again. And again. She blushes. A girl in my class giggles but tries to reassure the teacher that her mistake is okay and urges her to go on.

"Thank you Melissa", says Ms. Bethany and she continues. "So, when Frank first learns of this law...." the class erupts in laughter. Ms. Bethany gives up. "Continue reading on your own from chapter seven. I'll put questions on the board for you to answer, they are due at the end of class."

Ms. Bethany goes and sits at her desk. Ms. Bethany is young for a teacher and I guess she is okay looking. Typically she is a pretty good teacher, for the most part, we like her.

I start to read chapter seven and find I am easily distracted. I don't like this book. I read another paragraph and glance over at Ms. Bethany at her desk. She is looking up at the ceiling and then writing something down. It looks like she is looking for answers on the ceiling. She's concentrating hard on something. I give up trying to read the chapter and start to work on the questions she wrote on the board. I figure I can just thumb through the chapter and find my answers.

When I'm done with the assignment, I get up to bring it to her desk. I can see what she has been working on the whole class. On her desk is a piece of paper, across the top it says *Puerto Rico, Packing List*. She's got a huge list of what she needs, hair dryer, nail polish, bikini. *Bikini?* I shudder to myself. She may be young and okay looking, but one thing you never want to picture is your teacher in a bikini! Eww. Then, I notice something else, something I don't think was there before. Ms. Bethany has a shiny new diamond ring on her hand. It must be from Frank. I get it now.

Right after lunch, we all piled into the gym for the circus freaks show.

I sat with Thomas and we chatted about the new super hero movie he is going to see over vacation, as boring as Thomas can be, he is far more interesting than the juggling freaks.

The audience claps, I guess I missed something amazing that the freaks did, maybe one rode a unicycle or something. Whatever. I started to pay attention. The show was okay, but then came the best part; right in the middle of someone walking a portable tight rope they brought with them, we had a fire drill! Epic! The dude fell off the wire and kids spilled out of the gym into the field beside our school.

In the field, kids darted around, some sat in the grass, I saw a kindergartener crying. I guess the fire alarm had scared her. I would have been more incline to cry over the circus freaks, but whatever, she was still little. I wandered around outside waiting for the go ahead to go back into the school. Teachers were frantically running about trying to get a head count; since we hadn't been in our classes, there was no organization outside. I chuckled at the chaos.

"Hey! Rocket!" I heard James yell. Rocket's her nickname for me. I might as well explain. When we were seven years old, I came up with a great plan to build a rocket. I was going to launch the two of us right into space. We were going to be famous! The first kids ever to build a working rocket ship!

I guess I don't need to tell you, since I am not famous, that it did not work. James got the biggest laugh of her life and has called me Rocket ever since. Payback is painful.

"Rocket!" she yelled again and I followed the sound to find her under a tree looking at something.

"Check it out" she said. "I think its hurt." She crouched to the ground and I saw she had found a bird with what looked like a broken wing.

Now, say what you will about me, I may not be super smart or dress great or be the best skate border. Some may even say I have a chip on my shoulder. But, the fact is, I am a sucker for animals. All animals. Dogs, cats, birds, worms, you name it, I'll love it.

"Oh man!" I said as I bent down with her. "It looks like its wing is broken. Poor little dude."

"How do you know its a 'dude'?" James asked, I ignored her. I just knew. Leave it at that.

James made a little pouch with the bottom of her shirt and scooped up the bird and placed it gently in the pouch.

In the background I heard the dismissal bell, *we were free!* April vacation! However, because of the fire drill, everyone needed to head back inside to get their stuff to bring home.

More chaos, there were kids everywhere! Everyone was trying to be the first to start their vacation. Some kids were heading in, some were heading out to the busses or their parent's cars. James and I were focused on the bird.

"What should we do with it?" she asked me.

I thought for a second. "Follow me."

We walked against the tide of kids into the school and headed up the stairs to the second floor where the nurse's office was. I tried the knob and found it locked. This is where my keen observational skills came in handy.

I had seen the school nurse going into her office one day without her keys. She lifted up on the knob, jiggled it slightly and, Presto! The door swung open. She glanced back around the hall to be sure no one saw her secret and then she disappeared into her office. She did not see me watching her from a cracked open bathroom door.

I'm not sure why the nurses office needs a lock anyway. I mean really, what are a bunch of kids gonna steal? Tongue depressors? No thanks. So, thanks to my being in the right place at the right time, and my interest that week in detective work, I learned that I too could enter the nurse's office as I pleased. I never had until now. I used the nurses trick, I lifted up, jiggled, and...IN!

Chapter 2

Dr. Rocket

First, let me just say that the door jiggling trick is common knowledge. I mean, the nurse isn't exactly stealthy. But Rocket was so proud of himself, I let him think that he was the only kid in the school who could open a broken lock. Once he opened the door, I carried the bird inside.

I rarely go to the nurse. Her office is so small, it feels like it's closing in on me. A doctors' scale sat in a back corner. A small desk with a computer on it took up most of the square footage of the closet sized room. A twin size bed took up the remainder. A shelf held tongue depressors, bandages, and every other first aid thing you could think of. The room looked like a gridlocked city intersection. We set the bird down on the bed and examined it.

"How do we fix a broken wing?" Rocket asked.

"How should I know?" I replied. "We could put a splint on it," I suggested.

"Great idea! Can you find medical tape? I'll get tongue depressors!" Rocket sounded like an excited little boy on Christmas. See, Rocket is an odd boy. He goes around, making sure everybody thinks he is tough, but then he does stuff like volunteering for the ASPCA and donating food. I even let him believe he taught me how to skateboard.

I found the tape and placed it on the bed where the scrawny little bird lay in obvious pain. Rocket had flexed out the wing and started to make a splint around it. When it was complete, he picked up the bird and admired his handiwork.

"Perfect," he mumbled to himself.

"Looks good to me." I said "You have a place to keep him til he heals?"

"I guess." Rocket shrugged, still focused on the bird.

I heard the sound of the busses outside and glanced out the window, the busses had begun to leave. I could see the chaos inside the last bus of sixty screaming kids, anxious to begin their vacation, and then, I panicked.

"Rocket!"

"What?" He replied casually, still examining the bird.

"The busses! They're leaving! They're...they're gone!" I watched the last one pull away from the school.

I'm not typically prone to panic, but this day was different. My Dad had gone to Italy on business and had taken Mom with him. So guess who was elected to care for Nanny this week? That's right, me.

I was supposed to take the bus to the stop closest to her house. My mom had arranged for a taxi to meet me there and take me the rest of the way to her house. Nanny's nurse checked in on her three times each day, but Mom thought it would be a "great way to prove I was growing up" and stay with Nanny and help feed and dress her, care for her house, that kind of stuff. Really, it was a way out of feeling guilty for not taking me to Italy with them. This way they could say I was *with* an adult, but really, she was *with* me.

Nanny was Dad's mom and was sick with dementia. Dad kind of put it on Mom to take care of her, hire her nurses, check in on her, things like that. I don't think my Mom would have

minded a job like that, however, Nanny had the kind of dementia that made her scream obscenities at whomever was in her
presence, I mean bad ones, I mean, this woman would make
you cry. Dad stayed away mostly because he was embarrassed,
but he couldn't handle her very well either. I wasn't thrilled to
be given this "opportunity", but it was my responsibility and
I needed to be there. It was too far to walk, and I didn't have
enough money with me to take a cab the whole way.

Crap! Now what? I thought.

Chapter 3

Getting Home

It had begun to drizzle outside. "Great, now we have to walk home." I said. "I can't carry this bird, my skateboard and my backpack all the way home."

I could see James was panicked about the busses but I didn't want to get into it, sometimes she was so overdramatic.

"Chill" I told her. I mean we had bigger problems than busses, I needed help carrying all this stuff.

"We'll take turns carrying the bird." James said her voice agitated. "Wait here, I have to run to my locker and get the rest of my stuff, I'll be right back, you stay with the bird."

"Hurry up." I made sure to add. I wanted to start my vacation more than anyone, and already we were the last ones out of the school.

I moved to the window and watched as the crowd outside thinned and teachers were getting in their cars and leaving too, it didn't take long before the parking lot was just about empty. I guess teachers hate school as much as we do.

"Ha! Whaddaya know?" I thought out loud.

I went back over to the bird and watched it hobble along on the table.

"Whatcha thinkin little guy?" I asked and stroked its back. "Don't you worry one bit, we'll have you all fixed up and ready to fly soon." I looked at the clock. "Hurry up James, I want out of this dungeon." I said to myself. I looked back at the bird. "You poor wittle thing..."

James walked in. "Did you just say 'wittle'?

"No."

"Yes you did, I heard you say 'wittle' to the bird." She started cracking up.

Sometimes I can't stand James. "Let's just go." I said desperate to change the subject.

I scooped up the bird and we headed down the stairs. I needed to stop by my homeroom and grab my board. I fumbled with all I had to carry, but I managed and we walked toward the closest exit.

"Boy, this place is like a ghost town." James said.

I couldn't resist, I let out the most evil and loudest "MWUHAHAHAHA" I could. It echoed through the empty hall. I dropped my board and hopped on. It felt liberating to be able to do whatever I wanted in a teacher-less school.

"Give me that bird, if you're going to do that you idiot!" James demanded.

I hopped off my board. I hate when she's right. I didn't want to give up the bird, but I was running the risk of hurting him again. I bent down to pick the board up and we walked, careful not to disturb the bird.

"Weee're freeeeee!" James sang and she pushed the handle on the door.

It was locked.

The rain outside was really coming down now.

We turned and headed to the front door of the school. As we passed by the office, I noticed all the office ladies and the principal were gone too, I don't think I've ever seen the office completely deserted like that. It was weird.

We got to the door and I backed into it to push the crash bar with my butt but it didn't move. Locked.

"What the heck James? All the doors are locked!"

"There's still one more in the back of the cafeteria" she said. "Let's go try that one."

Chapter 4

Locked In!

I just *knew* stupid Rocket had taken too long getting his stuff, I just *knew* it! Now we were having trouble finding a way out of school and I had to find a way to get to Nanny's house! My heart was the only sound I could hear thumping in my ears. Mom and Dad would be so mad at me! I wanted to scream! Instead, I heard myself say; "There's still one more in the back of the cafeteria, let's go try that one." And off we went toward the back of the school.

Rocket was trailing behind me carrying his stupid skateboard in one hand, his backpack over that same shoulder and balancing the bird in the other hand. I was holding my binder and my books to my chest as my pace quickened toward the back of the school.

The school seemed so strange with no one in it. We headed down the Science hallway, and took the left down the English and Languages hall toward the cafeteria.

We have to pass the auditorium on the way to the cafeteria. When I was little, I made up a story in my head that the auditorium was haunted. Now that I'm big, I still can't shake the ghostly feeling I get when I pass by and can see nothing but black through the windows on the door, the lights are out, the ghost is in. It totally creeps me out. I never told anyone that.

It doesn't seem like I can walk any faster than I am, but when we pass the auditorium doors, my pace quickens. We head into the cafeteria. I push ahead of Rocket, I've *GOT* to get out of here! Plus, he's a little slow carrying that bird.

I run to the door beside the kitchen.

Locked.

I look at Rocket trying to hide the panic in my eyes, but I know they are the size of saucers. I thought he would make fun of me, but instead, his jaw drops open. Crap.

Chapter 5

Still Locked In

"Are you kidding me? Why do the doors lock from the inside? There has to be a fire law about that somewhere!" I was getting irritated. Bird, skateboard, backpack...too much to carry and I wanted out! I pushed past James to try the door myself. Nothing. I thought for a second, scanning the map of the school in my mind. There was one more door. "The auditorium, let's go."

James didn't move.

"Let's go!" I started toward the cafeteria entrance. I didn't hear her footsteps behind me. "Come on!"

She started walking. We crossed the cafeteria and headed left to the auditorium. They were right next to each other, with a bathroom in between.

I started to go in. It was really really dark in there. Really. Dark. I didn't want to say anything to James, but I was a little creeped out. I couldn't open the doors with the bird in my hand, so I asked James to go ahead of me. She didn't move.

"Go!" We've got to get out of this dump! Go try the door." She still didn't move. "What's the matter with you?" I didn't want to let on that a dark auditorium was too creepy for me, I'd never hear the end of it.

She got that *I've got an evil idea* look on her face. Sometimes I love that look, it makes my life interesting when she's scheming something for us to do. I didn't get that feeling this time.

Chapter 6

Ghosts in the Auditorium

I grabbed the handle and yanked. "After you..." I said. Rocket looked all weird. "What the heck? GO!" I tried to lean on him a little, he was frozen in place.

I heard his breath shake and he swallowed hard. He was afraid! I *knew* it! I had an important and instant choice I had to make, the decision bounced around in my head like a ping pong ball I couldn't catch, but I knew I needed to take control. Oh! I wanted *SO* bad to make fun of him, but if I did, we'd never get in there to try the door, and I wanted out of here as much as his did. I made my choice; I had to be mature. It was so hard.

In my best maternal voice I eased him in. "It's okay, Rocket, just right down the aisle and out the exit, go ahead, you can do it, I'll be right behind you" I could be his best cheerleader when I needed to be.

Rocket's shoulders rose, his back stiffened, he took a deep breath and in he went. I didn't follow.

"Sorry Rocket" I whispered to myself. I had been so nervous about the stupid auditorium, I suddenly realized I had to pee. I was doing my little "gotta go" dance in the hallway while I waited for Rocket to try the door. What seemed like half a second later, Rocket burst back through the auditorium door, his face was red and he was breathing hard!

"What the heck James? Where were you?"

"Um, I have to pee" was all I could think to say.

Breathlessly he said, "Doors locked."

Of course. I put my pointer finger up, right in his face. I couldn't think right now. "Wait right here" I said and ran into the girls room.

Chapter 7

Light Dawns on Marblehead

We were stuck. Trapped. Hostages. Prisoners in the one place I do my very best to avoid. I leaned against the cold hard cement wall and sank down to the floor. I took the bird out of my shirt and cupped him in the palm of my hands. "Well, little dude, looks like we're here for the week."

I could hear the rain on the roof outside, it was coming down hard. Thunder and lightening were becoming constant. When James returned, I asked "You have your phone?" not really knowing who to call.

"My phone! YES! My phone!" her eyes glazed over as she realized she had left it with her mother that morning to deliver with her suitcases to her grandmothers house.

"Crap! No. I don't have it." There was a brief moment of silence.

Thunder clapped outside and shook the building.

"Hey! The office, let's try the office phone!" James' face lit up with her idea. She took off running toward the office. I was a little slower moving, I still was carrying the bird and I'm not sure why, but I still picked up my backpack and skateboard and began to follow her, my pace quickened when I saw the office door open and James slip inside.

When I caught up to her, she was already holding the phone to her ear. She looked up at me with a look I've never seen on James' face. She was scared.

"It's dead."

"The rain" I whispered barely audible, "its knocked out the phone line." I didn't need to say it out loud, James was already thinking the same thing. She turned and looked out the window and watched the steady stream of rain pour down the plexiglass window as she dropped into the secretary's chair. James straightened her back, her face returned to normal.

"Whatdaya wanna do now?" she said matter of factly, she shrugged and clapped her hands together.

Chapter 8

It's All Rocket's Fault

R ocket was in a trance. He still cupped the bird in his hands but dropped his skateboard down on the floor.

"Whatdaya want to do?" I asked again. He didn't respond. "Rocket! You're the one who got us into this mess, what do we do now?"

"You're blaming ME?" he sounded surprised.

"Umm, yeah...you wanted to save the stupid bird, so ye-ah...I'm blaming you."

"You're kidding, right? James, you know I want to be out of this place more than anyone! How was I supposed to know the crappy doors locked from the inside?"

I could tell his ranting soliloquy was going to continue, so I brushed past him and walked out into the hallway trying the front door one last time.

I could see Rocket through the office hallway window having a brilliant conversation with himself. He was exasperated, yelling into the air. His one bird-less arm flailing.

I kept walking back to where I had dropped my backpack by the auditorium. I was thinking I'd left a granola bar in it. I was getting hungry.

Chapter 9

Whatever

I could not believe I was being blamed for this catastrophe! Whatever. Typical. Blame me. I swung open the office door not knowing exactly where I was going. I wandered the halls for a bit realizing that I was needing to find a place for the bird, so I headed for the science lab to find a container or a box of some kind. The rest of my stuff, backpack etc, I had left outside the office door.

I had no idea where James was, but finding her didn't even cross my mind. The science hallway was down the back right side of the building. The science part of the school had both traditional class rooms and labs.

I went into Mr. Kennedy's lab room. Each lab table had a sink and faucet at the end of it. I slid my hand under the bird inside my shirt and lifted it out, my hand felt greasy. "ARGH!!!" I yelled into the air at no one in particular. "STUPID BIRD POOPED ALL OVER MY SHIRT!"

This day got better and better by the minute! I lowered the bird into one of the sinks and went to another table to wash my hands and shirt. By the time I was done, I was soaked. Whatever.

My stomach began to growl, I hadn't eaten since lunch and that was at 11:45 and for whatever reason, I had eaten a light lunch today; I had only had 4 slices of pizza, a fruit cup, 3 containers of milk, a thing of potato puffs and a pudding, it was time to eat. The bird must be hungry too.

Shoot! I thought to myself, *now what?* I'm gonna starve to death in the most hated place in the world. What an ending. I could see the headlines now "Boy and his bird die of starvation over school vacation" Beautiful. I left the bird in the sink where he should be safe for a bit, and have a place to poop, and headed to the only place that I may find sustenance, the cafeteria.

Chapter 10

Rocket the Crooner

I grabbed all my stuff and headed back toward the office while munching my granola bar, I was taking small slow bites to savor what may very well be the only thing I would have to eat until someone could come get us out of this place.

A thought of my grandmother flashed through my mind and I felt a burning in my stomach, I couldn't think of that now, I needed to use all of my energy thinking of a way out.

I glanced in each class room as I passed them to see if maybe, just maybe I could catch someone still in the school.

Our school without people in it felt dead, strange, incredibly lonely. It was as if a student could give each desk life. I hadn't realized it before, but a person could actually *see* imagination at work. All the books in the school, without someone to read them were empty shells. Observing, or even just knowing someone was reading them brought them to life, as if you could see the imagination of the reader floating somewhere above their head, joining with other stories, mixing with other thoughts, mingling with other kids' creations to create a life, a living breathing entity inside this otherwise dead building. I shivered a little at the emptiness and quickened my pace back toward the main office to collect up Rocket. I didn't care what he had to say, it didn't matter anymore whose fault this was, we needed to find a way out. We needed each other.

When I arrived at the office, I saw he was gone. The building suddenly felt too big. I wanted to be with Rocket. I said his name and got no answer. I said it a little louder. Nothing.

Even though I knew we were the only people in the building, I had been so conditioned to not yelling in the school, I felt funny when I raised my voice only slightly to call his name again. He didn't answer. *Where the heck had he gone off to now? He had darn well better be in this building and not found a way out without me!* My thoughts raced.

Inside the office, I spun around not sure where to look or what do to next. My eyes fell upon the PA system. I flipped the "on" switch. I felt so guilty. I knew this was not something I was supposed to be doing, if it were a normal day, but I guess this was pretty far from normal, so I took a deep breath, leaned forward toward the microphone and spoke.

"Hello?" It barely squeaked out of my mouth. "R - Rocket?" I half expected an answer. "Where are you?" I was treating the machine as if it were a telephone, and I listened carefully for an answer. It never came.

I paced around the office for another ten minutes waiting for Rocket to arrive. He never did. I ran my finger along the edge of the secretary's desk. I played with a paperclip. I needed to go find Rocket.

I left my backpack on the secretary's chair and headed out to find him.

I had just come from the math hallway when I went to get my granola bar and I hadn't passed him there, so I went down the left side of the school, down the science hallway, glancing in each room as I went and calling his name. I reached the end of the hall way and turned right, that's when the cafeteria came into sight and I slapped myself in the forehead. *Of course!*

Food! Rocket can't go without for very long, he must be in the caf'. I giggled a little and pulled open the double doors.

"Rocket! You idiot! Where have you been?" I yelled into the empty room.

He didn't answer back.

"I swear to God, if you jump out at me, I'll kill you! Yes I will! Kill you dead! You KNOW I hate being jumped out at!" I walked slowly through the room. There really was no place for him to hide, the tables had been washed and folded up and pushed against the walls for their restful vacation. "Rocket! Come on! Jokes over! Where arrrrreeee you?" I yelled. Then I heard a sound. I stopped and listened. It sounded like the PA system, but there were no speakers in the caf'. I turned toward where it sounded like it was coming from and it led me back out to the hall.

"De be do be dooooo" Rocket crooned over the school PA system. "Doo doo be doo be. Ya ya la la laaaaa. "DOOOOO BEEEE DOOOO BEEEEE DOOOOO" he continued.

"Oh my God! ROCKET!!!" I yelled laughing into the air and raced back to the main office.

"You're the biggest dufas I ever met!!" I yelled as I ran.

Rocket is an idiot, but he has always made me laugh. Even when things were tough, like they are now. He can reach down and bring out his inner goofy-ness every time. He hasn't had it easy, I know this. Anything resembling a family life has eluded him his whole life.

My parents aren't even close to "normal" but I can say, they are much closer to it than what Rocket has at home. My mom works crazy hours and Dad goes away on business a lot, but Rocket's mom has been known to forget to come home at all. Rocket has never told me this, but I know. His mom is funny like he is, but I think she's more interested in whatever guy is in her life at the time than she is Rocket, she's lucky he is as self sufficient as he is, for a boy anyway. I mean, he still shows up for school every day unless he's sick, and his grades are okay.

They eat a lot of fast food in that house, subs, pizza, MacDonald's, Wendy's, but his mom does make the *best* peanut butter and fluff sandwiches I've ever tasted. She's made them for us for summer lunches when she is home. My mom would kill me if she knew I was eating that much sugar in one fist full, but it is *very* satisfying!

His mom treats us like we are her friends and talks about things my mom would *never* say, or probably has never even heard. She talks about money problems and man problems and she talks about her own mom as if she never existed! She tells me about the flaws on her own body and says things like "Well honey, if Mark doesn't like this caboose of mine...the heck with him! I'm not getting any younger ya know!"

She once brought Rocket and I along when she was bidding on some storage lockers. My mom still doesn't know that. There were people there that I can only describe as, as my mom would put it - bizarre. They were a crowd I never really knew existed, they all dressed really strange and smelled funny. I think they thought they were dressed nice, but the style was maybe, let's just say very outdated and some were a little extravagant.

I saw a woman there in heels so high, I think she could have touched the top of the empire state building! I saw men with shirt collars so wide, it looked like it was part of another shirt. There were people there in full leather! In the middle of the summer! Leather pants and jackets! There were young people and there were old people.

Anyway, Rocket's mom seemed to know what she was doing. She stood right up in front for some lockers and hid in the shadows for others. Sometimes she would ask us to stand real close to her and other times she'd ask us to pretend we didn't know her. She had her strategies, though I didn't understand them. Watching her was magical. She was smooth as silk, and ruthless. She was ruthless. She knew these people, knew their weaknesses and pounced! She almost always got what she came for, but if she didn't she was great at pretending it wasn't what she wanted anyway. The crowd loved her and hated her. It was another world.

My mom likes Rocket's mom "from a distance". She trusts me enough to hang out there anyway. I know she has helped her out with finding places to live, but I think its mostly because she cares about Rocket. She invites him over sometimes for dinner and once, to my complete embarrassment, bought him a winter jacket. It was getting late in fall and he was still trying to squeeze into the jacket he wore for the last two years. She told him a client had given it to her to give to me, but it was too "boyish", so she asked him if he would take it. Rocket never caught on, and was happy to have it. At least it wasn't from a storage locker.

"DOOO BEEE DOOO BEEE DOOOO!" he continued then changed his tune to some heavy metal song I didn't know. When I arrived and saw him through the glass, he was pretending to smash his guitar on the floor and all over the office.

Chapter 11

Planning the Excape (except it doesn't work)

66 **J** ames my friend." I said in my best British accent. I bowed and invited her into the office. "We are in luck," I couldn't wait to show her the bounty I had discovered in the cafeteria kitchen. "Follow me."

James couldn't contain her excitement. "What is it? An open door? What? What? Where are you taking me? Where are we going? What's going on? Is someone here?" God she could talk a lot. I just kept walking. She trailed behind me down the hall squaking question after question. "who, what, when, where, how?" On and on. Enough already.

I stopped in front of the commercial size refrigerator and pulled open both doors simultaniously. "TA DAAAA!"

"What?" asked James.

"What, what?"

"What am I looking at?"

I turned at looked at her in disbelief. "Are you kidding? This is all ours! Someone left the doors unlocked! Everything in here is for. The. Taking!!"

"Why couldn't they have left the school doors unlocked instead?"

"Really? How can you NOT be excited about this? This bounty laid out before us." I mumbled "there IS a God" under my breath as I reached for the pre-sliced bologna and shoved a piece in my mouth.

"Oh my God Rocket, we are actually stuck here aren't we?" I could see the realization come over her face and for a second I almost got sucked into it too. I decided to focus on the block of cheese slices.

Like her mood, James sunk down to the floor. She sat, holding her knees to her chest. She looked up at me for answers. I offered a hunk of cheese. She just shook her head.

"Your loss" I shrugged and shoved the cheese into my mouth. "If we're gonna be stuck here, we might as well make the best of it."

I knew James needed me to be different, tender even, but that's not me. I did my best. "Hey, did you hear about the Dad who asked his daughter for a newspaper? She said, Dad, we get our news on the iPad now, and she handed him the iPad. The fly never knew what hit him." I cracked myself up. "Did you know the wide mouth frog that hopped through the zoo asking every animal what they like to eat?"

"Enough Rocket!" said James. "I appreciate what you're trying to do, but I don't like this." The rain pounded the roof and the wind continued to blow. It was darker in the cafeteria than it normally was. "What are we going to do?" she was looking to me again for answers. I didn't have any.

"What were you supposed to do over vacation, weren't you spending it with your Dad's crazy mother? C'mon! How fun is that? We have this WHOOOLLLEEE building to ourselves! We can do ANYTHING! The possibilities are endless! Plus, there's more food here than I've ever seen in my lifetime! C'mon James." I reached down and offered her my hand to help her up. I was hoping she'd get up. Enough already. I didn't see this side of James often, and I didn't like it. Thankfully she took my hand and stood.

"We've got responsibilities, c'mon, stop being so selfish and thinking about yourself!" I said sarcastically. She looked puzzled.

"The bird James, the bird! Poor dude is starving! Quick, look around for bread, or crackers." She smiled and I felt relieved.

We headed down the hall and I showed James where I had left Max.

"Max?" James chuckled.

"Yes. Max." I said matter of factly. Fact was, I just made up the name the moment I said it.

Max took the crackers we had brought and ate hungrily. I was pleased he was eating, and happy we were able to help him and keep him out of the torrential rain outside.

James walked out of the room and I followed.

"What are you doing?" she was rummaging in a closet in the art room.

"Come on, help me, I'm making a sign."

"A sign? What for?" for whatever reason, the only thing that came to mind was a lemonade stand sign, and I was pretty sure that we weren't going to be selling much lemonade here, in the school, empty, and alone. James just told me I was numb above the ears and continued to pull out paper, tape, poster board and paint.

"Grab whatever you can." she instructed me. We spent the next hour making signs for the windows. They said different things, but all basically had the same message; the signs were alerting the public that drove by that we were stuck inside. All that was fine and good, and would have been a terrific idea if our school wasn't on it's own private drive. The only reason for anyone to be on this street is to come to the school, but it made James feel better, so I went along, besides, what else did I have to do.

We were on the second floor of the school hanging our last sign when a car actually pulled down the long winding street in front of the school. It stopped right at the front door in the bus lane.

"Saved! Thank you, God!" I said.

James and I couldn't believe our luck! A kid got out and ran through the rain up to the front door, found it locked and returned to the car.

James and I both pounded on the window and screamed as loud as we could through the tiny crack the window was allowed to open. (I guess the reason the windows didn't open more than a crack was that they didn't want any kids flinging themselves out a window to an early death just because they didn't do their math homework or something. Adult thinking was weird. Whatever.)

With the sound of the rain pounding on the roof of the car, and pounding the pavement and pounding the building, there was no way they were going to hear us. We saw the driver get out, but they had an umbrella preventing them from looking up and seeing us.

We bolted towards the stairs. I slid down the first bannister, James took the stairs one at a time, but her feet were moving so fast, she reminded me of the Sherpa's in the Hymalayas we had learned about. They would guide mountain climbers up the mountains, and they never grew tired while climbing. The secret was the fast tiny steps they took, while their backpacking counterparts were exhausted a half mile in. Those little Sherpa dudes were genius!

I took the next flight two and three steps at a time and beat James to the front door. I got there just in time to see the car's tail light growing smaller and dimmer as the car drove out of sight. "AAARRRGGHHHH!" I pounded my fist on the doors plexiglass window.

James was breathless "What happened? Where'd they go? Why didn't you stop them? Are they coming back?" Again with the questions.

"They're gone." I said, my forehead pressed against the plexiglass. I turned and walked, where was I going, I had no idea.

Chapter 12

Getting Comfortable

It was getting late in the day and becoming more and more clear that we were not going anywhere. I sat by the front door for quite a while, worried that another car may come and we may miss it. My brain hurt from thinking. I should have been hungry by now but strangely, I wasn't. I sat a bit longer.

The storm continued to thunder outside. I got up and decided to walk to my home room. I thought I should probably make a "home base" for myself and home room felt like the natural choice.

We had a corner with a carpet and about 8 bean bag chairs, it was cozy enough, for a school at least. I collected up everything that was mine and headed there. I walked in and flipped on the light, it felt too bright. We had a nice floor lamp on the carpeted section, so I turned that on and shut off the overhead fluorescents. I let my bag slip to the floor and a plunked into the gray bean bag.

I looked around the room trying to soak up everything I never noticed about the room before. One doesn't typically contemplate a school room, they walk in on the first day, glance around, find a seat and that's about where observation ends. I looked around the room like I had never seen it before, it was familiar, and it wasn't. My mind felt blank.

I looked up and behind me and noticed all of the different books in the bookshelf behind me. I closed my eyes, reached behind and picked a book. I was an avid reader, I loved books, just about all of them. I have pretty eclectic taste in books. I've been know to read science fiction, travel, poetry, Greek mythology and cultural books, but I do hate love stories.

I don't know if liking romance is something I'll grow into, or just part of my personality, but honestly, I don't get it. I mean, they are so far from reality. I chuckled at the thought, I mean, it was easier for me to believe in an established colony on an asteroid where the population is all teenagers because they were the only ones to survive our own atmosphere releasing poisonous gases and having the werewithall to build a craft to propel themselves into the depths of outerspace and create a livable habitat on a rock, than it was to believe in two people who never argue, who get lost in each others eyes, who dream of prom dates or weddings and live happily ever after. I mean, it just doesn't happen.

My mom used to laugh when she would tell me about when I was little and how I hated to be read stories like *Cinderella*, or would only let her read *Snow White* until midway through the dwarf part. I knew a handsome prince was coming and I couldn't stand the thought. I would much rather her read to me *What it's like to be a Chicken* or *Look into the Deep, Everything You Want to Know about Sharks*.

The book I grabbed was called *Robbie and Me*. A love story. Of course. I opened the cover and shrugged. I thought I'd give it a try and see if I had matured any. I hadn't. I got about three chapters in and couldn't do it. I closed the book, put it down and felt the need to cleanse my brain with a good sci-fi. I rolled out of the bean bag to find one.

Once again Rocket came over the loud speaker. "James

Whittimore, please report to the gymnasium." He was using his best serious voice. "James Whittimore, to the gymnasium, please." he clicked it off.

"Oh please tell me he found a way out." I whispered. I glanced at the clock, it was nearing 7pm. I headed to the gym, on his instructions.

I arrived at the gym about three-seconds before he returned from the office. I peered into our gym and was whispering "Oh my God, what did you do?" when he appeared suddenly behind me.

"TA DA" he said and swung his arm out like the models do in game shows. "Whaddaya think?"

"What is it?" I asked scanning the gym equipment scattered in some sort of ordered pattern all over the floor.

"An obstacle course." he said as if it was obvious. "Check it out..." he raced into the gym to demonstrate.

"Where did you find all this stuff?" I laughed.

"Look." He pointed "Mrs. Cutler's office is open."

"Seems like every door was left open except..."

"Come on, let me show you" he interrupted to keep me off the subject of us being stuck.

He had certainly been busy. He seemed most excited to show me what was in his hand. "Check it out, her stop watch! It was in her desk's top drawer. Since we can't go through it at the same time, we can time each other and whoever has the best time, wins."

Rocket was such a child sometimes, but he could really be fun when he wasn't acting stupid. And, to be honest, it looked like he put a lot of effort into this and it kind of looked cool.

"First", he explained "you have to kick all five balls into the net, then you run over here. Pick up the Frisbees and try to get them through the basketball nets, which, you will never be able to do, by the way. Then you come to this section."

He had laid out the huge park ball. The thing came up to my

waist and when you bounced it, it went so high and bounced so slow, and made the funniest sort of a *ke-ploonk* sound.

"You bounce the ball while you run putting one foot inside each hula hoop on the floor. Then you crawl through the tunnel, walk across the balance beam, run up to the top of the bleachers, across the top and down the other side. But FIRST, you must do the dizzy bat for 10 seconds."

He wanted me to put my forehead on the end of a baseball bat, the other end of the bat on the floor and spin around the bat for ten seconds and then try to run up bleachers? I was going to kill myself on this part, but I continued listening.

"Finally, you come over here flip over this bar and land on the puffy matt. At which time, I will stop the clock. Are you ready?"

"What? Wait....no!"

"GO!"

"Rocket!" I yelled as I began to run toward the first station. "I wasn't re-eddy!" My voice bounced as I ran.

I successfully kicked all 5 balls into the net, years of soccer finally paid off. I flung the Frisbees around and mostly they bounced off the backboards. Bouncing that big ball took some getting used to, there was a rhythm to it, but I caught on pretty quick. Tunnel, balance beam, dizzy bat, bleachers, flip and whoosh, I was lying on the big puffy mat, breathless and a little dizzy.

"Not bad, not bad" Rocket said with a little sarcasm. "43.2 seconds. Now, check this out, here, time me," he said handing me the stopwatch.

Chapter 13

James Lies

J ames is such a sore winner. First of all, I know she didn't click the stopwatch right away each time I tried, she cheats like that. Whatever. I know I beat her all three times we ran the course.

Now the problem was two of the Frisbees I flew got stuck in the rafters. Mrs. Culter was *very* particular about her equipment, if I didn't get them down, I was as good as dead. I swear she'd fingerprint everyone in the school to find who did it. I had to get them down. I wasn't exactly sure how.

"Rocket, I'm starving! James's voice broke my concentration. "I'm heading to the cafe now. When you get over losing to me, come eat," and she walked out.

I joined her and we dined on bologna, cheese, crackers and some frozen pizza we found, then it seemed like it was time to settle in for the night. That was an odd thought to have in your own school.

I felt restless, bored. I wasn't sure where I belonged overnight. I went to check on Max. His head was tucked under his good wing, even he was in for the night. I didn't want him to be alone, so I hopped up one of the lab tables and lay staring at the ceiling.

James had gone to her homeroom to read for a while. The school made sounds at night. There was banging and clunking and a soft whirling sound that was barely audible. It didn't bother me, having moved so many times, I guess I was used to each house having their own sounds, and more often than not, I was used to being alone at night. James wasn't. She was used to familiar places, soft sheets and pillows and someone to kiss her good night. This is what I was thinking as I lay on the hard table top. This is what I was thinking when James whispered from the doorway. "Rocket? You awake?"

"What's up?" I said still looking at the ceiling. There was an annoyance to my voice, I didn't mean it.

"This is weird."

"What's weird?"

"This"

"What?" I laid still.

"This" now she was starting to sound slightly annoyed.

I rolled over to face her, still in the doorway. "What?"

"This whole thing." She was wringing her hands as she struggled to find the words to describe what *this* was. "Sleeping in the school."

"I sleep in school every day." I said and rolled back, face up again.

"That's not what I mean and you know it! It's too big here, there's too many rooms. I hear noises, its creepy a little and...."

"So, what do you want me to do about it?" that was cold, I didn't mean it.

"I don't know," she paused "How's the bird?" I guess she had given up on me having the answers to the school sleeping arrangements.

I didn't roll over, I just pointed over my head at the sink where Max was sleeping. I heard her walk over.

"Oh, he's sleeping. How sweet!" She stood in silence for a second or two, it felt longer. "OK, I'm going back to my room now."

"Night" I said.

"Night."

I lay there in the dark for a while until sleep took over. I woke once in the night when my head dropped into the sink at the end of the table, I slid back down and rolled over. The sound of the thunder shook the building and even though I was on the first floor, I could hear the rain continue to pound on the roof. I drifted off again.

Chapter 14

The Arrival of Saturday

The night was long and difficult. The thunder woke me more times than I could count. It was cold and uncomfortable. I had lined up the bean bag chairs into a sort of bed, but each time I tried to get comfortable, they slid apart from each other and I would fall through the crack, so I curled up on the carpet.

I was never so happy to see morning.

The sun rose but did not shine, the heavy rain continued. I walked over to the window and watched the patterns the water made as it ran down the plexiglass panes. I felt a little embarrassed thinking this way at my age, but I really wanted my mommy. I said it just like that in my head *I want my mommy.*

I was wondering where in the world she could be right now. Probably waking to the smell of coffee and breakfast being cooked and served right in the restaurant of the hotel. I pictured it bright and sunny where she was. I pictured her in bed with the sunlight streaming through the window as she slowly sat up and stretched and smiled.

Holy cow, I think I just wrote a coffee commercial in my head! In the next scene, my mom would be looking out of the hotel window holding a warm cup of coffee with both hands while my Dad hugged her from behind.

Okay, enough of that. I needed breakfast, and to find a way out of here. I made my way to the office the try the phones again, they were still dead. I wondered if they would ever be fixed if no one knew they were broken. *Do phones just turn back on again like the electricity does after the storm passes?* I wondered. I lifted each receiver in the office and listened to the same sound of nothing. Worse than nothing, there was a sound to it, an indescribable sound. A sound like a heart monitor makes when someone dies, there is still a sound, but no life. But even heart monitors had a sound, the phone didn't. It was an empty tunnel.

I headed for the cafeteria. From the office, I could have gone either way down the hall, the cafeteria was in the back of the building, for whatever reason, I took the south side hall. This simple error in judgement brought me by the doors to the auditorium. The haunted auditorium. I quickened my step as I went by and I gave myself goosebumps, but nevertheless, I arrived safely in the cafeteria.

I banged around awhile opening each and every cabinet door looking for something that resembled breakfast. I know some schools serve breakfast to their students, ours didn't, so I had to be pretty inventive here with what I had to work with. "Bread, ah ha! Bread makes toast." I said out loud like I was a detective finding new clues to my case. I had a brilliant idea. "Tater puffs! Yes! Frozen tater puffs! Now we're talking breakfast!" I stood with a loaf of bread in one hand and an industrial sized bag of frozen potatoes in the other. I slowly turned around looking at the canvass on which I was to paint this picture of breakfast. No toaster. *And how exactly do they cook these tater puffs?* Crap. It was too early to think.

"The oven. OK, I can do this. I'll turn on the oven". I found the temperature control knob and turned it up to 200, that seemed hot enough for potatoes, I mean, I know when we go to the ocean and the temperature is 85 my mom always says "You can fry an egg on the sidewalk today!" 200 seemed right.

I found a cookie sheet and poured the potatoes onto it and put it in the oven.

I hopped up on a counter and sat, waiting for my potatoes. I waited. And I waited. And I waited. And I waited some more. I remembered; *A watched pot never boils,* and for the first time, understood exactly what that meant. I decided to use the ladie's room.

Before I went back to the cafe, I splashed some water on my face and swished some around in my mouth. I straightened my hair with my fingers, cleaned the gunk out of my eyes, washed my hands and went back to eat.

I couldn't believe the potatoes were still cold! I hopped back up on the counter and waited some more. I looked up to see Rocket. He was yawning and his face was all screwed up funny. His hair looked like he just pulled his finger out of an electric socket. "Whatcha doin"? he asked mid yawn.

"Starving." I answered.

His face perked up. "What are you making?" he said full of excitement.

"Tater puffs" He pulled open the oven door to have a look. "They almost done?"

"No, they've been in a while and they're still cold."

Rocket shut the oven door and glanced at the temperature. "James you big dummy, 200 degrees won't cook these!" and he spun the control.

I was embarrassed a little. I could beat Rocket at most games, was a better skate boarder than he was, got better grades, was clearly a better obsticle course runner than he was, but when it came to cooking, my mom usually did it all. Sure, I helped peel carrots or chop onions, but she took care of the oven stuff. Rocket usually had to make dinner for himself or for his mom too because she would come home late. Cooking was Rocket's thing, not mine.

"There, I cranked it up, they'll be ready soon. What else we got here?"

I shrugged. "I couldn't find anything else - *breakfasty.*"

"Nonsence." he said and began to gather ingredients. I have to admit, we had a decent meal; fried bologna, tater puffs, toast (which he toasted in the oven) and peanut butter. We had milk and juice too.

"How's the bird?" I asked

"Max?"

"OK, how's Max?" I wasn't sure why Rocket was insistent on bird formalities, I would think just referring to him as "the bird" Rocket would know exactly *which* bird I was talking about.

"He's good. Gonna bring him more food after this." He gestured to his plate.

Chapter 15

James is Insane

I made us a monster breakfast! I don't mean to brag or any-thing, but I can **rock** a kitchen. James should have been extremely grateful she was trapped in here with me!

After breakfast, we went to feed Max. "Maximillion ol boy!" I declared upon entering the science lab. I could feel James roll her eyes behind me.

"Hey! Check it out!" Max had been pecking away at the wing splint we had made. "He wants it off."

"Should we take it off?"

"I think it should stay on at least another day." I put the food in front of him hoping it would stop him from the pecking. It didn't.

"Max! Come on, cut it out!" I slid my hand around and under his belly and lifted him up, he didn't like it. He started waving his wing around and thrashing in my hand. I put him on the lab table, he stopped thrashing but I could tell he was stressed.

"Maybe we should take it off." James suggested.

"Na, I know what I'm doing. One more day."

James bent over close to examine the bird. He examined

her back. She reached her hand out slowly and began stroking the birds head. He seemed to enjoy it. I stuck out my hand to do the same and he came at me with his beak open, ready to strike. "What the heck?"

James was bent over whispering to Max and scratching his head. "It's OK, you're gonna be OK, give it another day and we'll take it off, OK? What's that you say?" she leaned her ear in "You want me to tell the boy what?"

James is such a goofball.

She stood and looked at me funny.

"What?" I asked.

"She's ticked off."

"Who's ticked off?" *What the heck was she talking about?*

"She's ticked off." She jutted her chin toward Max. "She wanted me to tell you, she thinks you're an idiot."

"Why? What did *I* do?" I couldn't believe I was having this conversation as if the bird was really speaking! I swear, James made me crazy.

"She's a *girl*, Rocket. A G-I-R-L. A girl. She's a girl bird and you've been calling her Max. She's not happy." James had her hands on her hips and her foot was tapping on the floor.

"Are you crazy? You are, you know. There is no way on this earth that you can tell that that bird is not a boy bird."

"I'm calling her Sara. Sara, with no 'h'. Sara is her name. Isn't that right Sara?"

James scratched the birds head and it responded.

"What the heck?" I whispered under my breath. I will never understand girls.

James scooped up Max and started for the door. I let them leave. Whatever.

Chapter 16

Riding the Board

I gave Sara a tour of the school. Being a bird and all, I didn't think she'd ever have this opportunity again. I showed her the math hall, the language hall, the art room, she seemed to like all of the colors in there. I thought, her world must be full of color! Flying all around, she got to see trees and oceans and fields in a way I never would be able to.

We hung out in the art room for a while. The rain pounded at the window, there was no color today, only black and gray. I was glad she was safe, warm and dry here with me.

We left the art room and I carried her into the library. I selected a book and sat in the arm chair in the back corner of the room. I put Sara on the arm of the chair. The book I chose was *The Rainbow Fish*, obviously it was too young for me, but I thought Sara would appreciate the colors and the simple language. Plus, she probably didn't get to see a lot of fish. I read allowed to her. My sweet bird friend.

Soon, I heard wailing in the hallway, not scary wailing, more like a Tarzan yell. I put the book down and looked at Sara. "Wait here, I'll be right back." she strutted back and forth on the arm of the chair.

I ran into the hallway. "What the heck are you doing?" I laughed.

Rocket was lying on his stomach on his skateboard flying down the hallway at top speed. When he got to the end of the hall way, he turned the board to face the next hall, he positioned himself up close to the wall and, using his legs as springs, pushed off the wall and went screaming down the south hallway. I ran after him laughing.

"Give me a turn! Let me try!"

He turned down the next hallway, I kept running.

He had positioned himself crooked and I finally caught up to him when he crashed into the lockers on the left side. I was cracking up. He was moaning. "Are you OK?" I laughed.

"Ohhhhhh" he said rubbing his shoulder.

"Seriously," I tried to stop giggling incase he was really hurt. "You OK?"

He jumped up. "I'm fine." He tried to smile at me. His face was red and his mouth was all scrunched up, I knew he was trying to be brave. I've seen this face before.

"Let me have a turn."

He flipped up the board and handed it to me. I put it on the floor, stood on it, and rode it back to the end of the hall. I laid on the board and pushed off the wall with my feet. "Thiiissssss iiiissss sooooooo coooooollllll!" I laughed as I went zooming past Rocket who stood rubbing his shoulder.

We stayed in that hall a while practicing different ways to ride up and down the hall. On one hand it was really cool to have such a smooth place to ride, there were no bumps or pebbles or anything. On the other hand, without the bumps, even the subtle bumps of concrete, there was no friction, the board went super fast and felt a little slippery. Rocket fell a couple of times, but he bounced pretty well, so he was okay.

When that got old, Rocket announced he was hungry. What else is new? That boy was *always* hungry.

"Where's Max?" he asked

"Sara? She's in the library. I'll go get her." I walked back into the library. Sara had hopped down onto the seat of the chair. She looked happy to see me. "Come on Sara, let's get you some lunch." I scooped her up and went to join Rocket.

When I got to the caf, he wasn't there. I yelled his name a couple of times and finally he appeared.

"Hey! Guess where *you've* never been?" he was strutting, I knew he was proud of something he found or did.

"Where?" "The teachers lounge. I was just in there."

"Cool" I wasn't sure how to respond. I couldn't have been less thrilled.

"They got vending machines in there."

"Cool" I was still under impressed.

"With food in them" he was really working hard at getting me to respond as if he had discovered gold or something.

"Cool." I shrugged.

"Really James, that's all you can say? I found more food! Junk food! They have chips and toaster pastries and granola bars!"

"That's great Rocket, but you forgot one thing, we don't have any money."

His face fell flat. I could see him searching for an answer. "We could rock it until something falls out." That was his brilliant solution.

"Rocket, did you know 13 people a year die from vending machines falling on them? I am NOT rocking it."

He looked dejected. His brain was still working though, I could tell. This would not be the last time we would have the vending machine conversation.

Chapter 17

The Great Escape
(and it still doesn't work)

Whether James realized it or not, at some point, I was going to have that bounty of delicacies from the vending machine. Whatever.

After lunch I found the janitors closet and gathered up some tools, I don't know why I didn't think of this sooner, sometimes I was surprised by my own brilliance! I found a screw driver a hammer and some pliers and brought them to the door on the north side of the school.

I examined the set up of the handle and locking system, I thought, if I could remove the handle, it would release the lock and we would be free. The screws were Phillips head and I only had a flat head screw driver so it took an extra long time to get the screws out. One by one out they came.

I was getting excited, I couldn't wait to see the look on James' face when I got us out of here.

I was working on the last screw when the exterior handle fell off, I heard it hit the ground outside. The side I was working on came off in my hand. I gave the door a push. Nothing. *What?*

How could that be? There was now a gapping hole in the door and it was still locked!

I stood up and backed down the hall a few feet. I ran as fast as I could at the door, slamming it with my shoulder.

"OW!" I forgot, that was my bad shoulder, the one I hurt earlier skateboarding. I must have yelled pretty loud because James came running.

"Rocket! What are you doing!"

I was ramming the door with my butt. "Trying to get this door open!"

Without my asking, James starting barreling into the door too.

"Its not moving!" I said through my teeth. We gave it a valiant effort. Out of exhaustion, we both sat on the floor, trying to catch our breath.

James was the first to speak. "Rocket, I love you for trying, but really, you are an idiot." She motioned toward the door and the large hole I had created.

Rain was coming in so fast, the floor below had a pretty good sized puddle. I got up and tried to put the handle back in the hole but it wouldn't stay. Without the other side, which was now on the ground outside, it wasn't balanced and just kept falling out.

James had gone to the janitors closet to get some rags or whatever she could find. We stuffed the hole with rags and walked away.

There wasn't much to do, and I found myself wandering. I walked into a classroom, English room I think, I didn't know, I didn't have a class here. I sat at the teachers desk and looked out at the rows of empty desks. I started "teaching." I said to the empty room; "OK class, everyone better have their homework done, or you all fail! That's right, I said fail. An F for the year. In fact, let me get my grade book out right now..."

I opened the top drawer of the desk and reached inside.

There were pens and pencils and a box of staples and, what to my wondering eyes should appear...but, three quarters.

This was the dawning of my next brilliant idea!

I grabbed up the quarters and ran to the next classroom and opened that teachers drawer. I found two dimes and six pennies. I ran to the next room and the next and the next.

Most drawers yielded nothing, but it was worth the exploration.

I ran into the art room and found James and Max. I didn't speak, I went directly to the desk at the front of the room and started rummaging like all the others before, in that skinny little drawer in the middle. Sometimes I found what I was looking for at the top, sometimes at the bottom.

"What are you doing?" James asked and wondered toward me.

"Money." It was a simple answer.

"What do you mean, money?"

"Money. There's money to be found in these desks."

"Rocket, that's stealing!"

"That is not stealing, that's survival, my friend, survival."

"What are you talking about? We're surviving just fine!"

"And now, we are surviving with chips and toaster pastries!" and I showed her what I had collected.

"What are you talking about?" She was irritated.

"The vending machine James, we now have access to the stuff in the vending machine!"

"Oh my God!" was all she uttered and rolled her eyes. After a few seconds she said, "Really Rocket? You're really going to take people's money so you can have a bag of chips? What's wrong with the potato chips in the kitchen?"

She didn't understand anything.

"Those are potato chips, the vending machine has Doritos, and I think they were Cool Ranch Doritos."

She rolled her eyes and moaned. Whatever. I was one happy dude.

In the teachers lounge, I found I had enough for two things. I got my Doritos and a blueberry toaster pastry and I scarfed them down, I wasn't about to share them with the doubter in the art room!

I made for the gym to shoot some hoops. I grabbed a ball and began dribbling. I took a most excellent shot, I had more style and grace in my layup than anyone else had in their pinky finger. I missed. Whatever. I ran for the ball and took a shot from the end of the key, that's when they caught my eye.

The Frisbees were still in the rafters, I had to get them down or die trying.

Chapter 18

A Few Surprises

I wanted to surprise Rocket with a nice, or at least decent dinner. I found some fruit that I cut up and put in a fruit salad for dessert. In the big walk-in freezer I found some chicken and there were always potato puffs. I found lettuce and tomatoes and chopped them up for a salad. I knew enough to defrost the chicken in the microwave, that was easy enough, there was a button specifically for that. I also knew from Rocket that the oven should be at least at 350 degrees. I found barbeque sauce and poured it over the chicken and dumped the puffs onto a cookie sheet and threw it all in the oven. Again, I waited. I was hoping Rocket wouldn't show up because I really wanted this to be a surprise. In fact, I was the one who was surprised when the kitchen began to fill up with such delicious smells, I was rather proud of myself. When it looked to be all done, I went to find Rocket. I yelled his name as I walked up and down each hallway and got no answer. I arrived at the gym and found Rocket just in time.

"What the heck Rocket, now what are you doing?"

"James! Grab the ladder, it just fell!" Rocket was hanging 20 feet in the air from the rafters.

He had pulled a desk type table into the gym and on top of that, put a folding chair and on top of that, a small ladder that had slipped off the chair.

He was hanging by his hands and swinging his legs up to try and grab the rafters with his ankles.

I grabbed the ladder and climbed up onto the table and repositioned the ladder and held it steady as he balanced on the top step and climbed down. "I'm sure I don't have to tell you how stupid that was."

"Shut up James."

"What were you doing?"

"Getting the Frisbees down."

"Oh, the Frisbees." I totally understood. I knew Mrs Cutler just as well as Rocket did and I had to say, death ladder and all, those Frisbees needed to come down.

We stopped talking. We had a silent understanding of what had happened here. We walked together back to the kitchen and that's when we saw the smoke.

We began to run.

"What the heck James?"

"I was trying to make dinner, I guess I forgot to take it out of the oven." I yelled to Rocket.

Rocket ran ahead of me and grabbed some pot holders, he fanned the fumes and bravely reached into the oven to remove the charred remains of my dinner. "What was it?"

"Doesn't matter" I said. Just then, the fire alarm sounded.

Normally, I hate the loud shrill of the fire alarm, but Rocket and I had the same thought at the same time. "The Fire Department!" we both chimed in unison.

"Quick, run around the school and pull every fire alarm!" Rocket instructed, and we did.

I was so overjoyed! We were going to get out of here! Rocket ran one way, I went the other, we pulled them all. It was glorious fun! As I ran down the main hallway, I saw Rocket down the other end, he had stopped running and was walking. "What's the matter?" I yelled.

"James, the phones are dead," he yelled back.

"I know, so what?" I bellowed over the shrieking alarm.

"The alarms are connected to the phone system. If the fire department doesn't get a call, they don't come!"

"Crap. Then how do we get it to shut off?" I was so frustrated at the noise now.

"It should shut itself off in a few minutes." Rocket explained, and it did. It was the worst silence I had ever heard.

Rocket and I spent the next several days exhausting every possibility of ever getting ourselves out, this was our April vacation, we should be home enjoying it.

It was that night, the night of the fire alarm, that I spent it in the art room with Sara. I had created a nest type bed for her with some cotton batting I found in the supply closet. She continued to peck at her bandage.

When the next morning arrived, I automatically looked in her "nest" and she wasn't there. Her bandage was, but Sara was gone. I heard the sound of beating wings and looked up. Sara was on top of the art supply closet, she could fly! It was time to let her go.

The rain outside had finally tapered off to a heavy fog. I was able to coax Sara down and carried her to go find Rocket, who continued to spend his nights in the science lab for whatever reason.

There was a couch in the library that would have been much more comfortable but Rocket wasn't really the library type, maybe he didn't even know it was there. I made a mental note to mention it to him later.

"Rocket, say good bye to Sara"

"What?" He was awake when I found him, but still very groggy.

"Its time to let her go, she can fly now."

We opened the window as far as it would crack out and we unceremoniously let her go.

"Bye Sara" I said.

"See ya, Max" said Rocket. "Stay cool," and he thumped his chest with a closed fist.

I released the bird and watched her fly down to the ground. She hopped around for a minute and then took off for a tree. I watched as she became swallowed up by spring's new leaves.

She was gone. I was so glad we could help.

We spent most of the rest of the day playing cards we found in the after school program game box. Sometimes we'd get restless and wander the halls for a while.

I did mention the couch to Rocket, he didn't seem to be interested. I decided to sleep there myself.

Chapter 19

Our Fearless Leader, The Principal

The first few days stuck at school went by so slowly, the next few flew.

James spent a lot of time reading and I spent a lot of time in the gym, making sure each time to put away any equipment I used.

By Tuesday morning when I woke I was starting to feel stir crazy. The weather outside had broken and I could see sun. I was also getting really tired of the food choices in the cafeteria.

I met up with James.

"James? Why do my teeth feel like they're wearing sweaters?"

"Rocket, haven't you been at least trying to wash in the bathroom?"

"Ummmm." I didn't really have an answer, or at least, I didn't want to answer her.

"I take a paper towel and wet it and wipe my teeth off with it. I wash my face and hands every day."

I shrugged. I guess it never crossed my mind. Whatever.

"You're disgusting." and she gave me one of her girly punches in the arm.

Tuesday afternoon we were on the second floor in the back corner of the school playing Monopoly when I got that feeling again. Something just felt different, off. I sat up straight with the dice in my hand.

"Go." said James, I didn't move.

"Go" she said again. I didn't move. I was listening, but I wasn't sure for what.

"Shhhhh." I told her.

"What?" She half whispered.

I held my finger to my lips and waved my left hand in a downward motion to get her to shut up. I heard something.

"Rocket, you're freakin me out! What's going on?"

I stood and walked to the doorway and stuck my head out. I heard something. I wasn't sure what it was.

"Someone's here!" I said breathlessly and I took off down the hallway.

I got to the front of the school, still on the second floor and ran into a classroom. I ripped off the sign we had taped to the window and looked below. Indeed, there was a car by the front door, its engine running. I opened the window the six inches it would open and yelled out. "HEY!"

The car was the one I thought our principal drove, kind of a geeky car, not very sporty, just kind of square, much like him. I bet it went 0-60 in 4.5 minutes.

I ran back out of the room and down the hall to the stairwell. About half way down the stairs I could hear humming. He was in the building all right! I jumped to the bottom of the stairs and ran as fast as I could toward the front of the school and the office.

I was no more than fifty feet from the front door when I heard his key in the lock. I picked up speed. "NO!" I yelled! "WAIT!" but he didn't. He locked the door behind him and hopped in his car. I pounded on the plexiglass like I had before. "WAIT!!! DON'T LEAVE!" Oh my God, this was hopeless.

I suppose if your in a place you don't expect anyone else to be, you don't necessarily listen for sounds of other people. He never heard me. James didn't even make a run for it. She told me she thought for sure I would find the person in the building and come back for her. She had stayed behind and started to clean up Monopoly. Terrific. I had been winning. Thanks James.

Chapter 20

The Book Castle

By Wednesday of vacation week I had spent more time in the library than I had in my entire life. I had read so many books and half books and chapter titles. One time Rocket came in and actually asked me to read to him. I did for a little while but he was so busy fiddling with books, he wasn't really listening.

He would pick up the hardcover books and pretend the covers were wings and he "fly" them around the room like they were airplanes. Real mature Rocket. So, I stopped reading. He picked up another book and balanced it on top of the first book, then he balanced another. It was like a house of cards, only with books.

That look came over his face again, he was having one of what he calls his 'brilliant ideas'.

"James! We've got thousands of books here!" He looked kooky eyed around the room.

"Boy, nothing gets by you Rocket. What are you thinking?"

"Grab some, lets build a fort!"

"A fort?"

"Yeah, a fort, with rooms and hallways and secret passages."

I felt a pang of guilt for all the books being taken off the shelves, but it did sound kinda cool and we had run out of ideas of things to do. So I agreed. It was more difficult than it sounded.

We didn't just pile books on top of books, we would have run out too quick if we did that. We had to stand them on end and balance them on top of each other.

We build a main room in the library but we were running out of space, so we expanded it out into the hallway.

We created crawl spaces and rooms. Rocket even made furniture with some of the books. We stacked them all just so and used the paperbacks for a roof.

The library was on a corner of the school, so we were able to expand into two hallways. If you entered from the left side, there was an actual human-sized doorway that opened up into a living room where Rocket had put the chairs he built. From there, you would have to get on your hands and knees and crawl through the library doorway into two other large rooms that were adjacent to each other.

If you entered from the other hallway, you'd have to do so on your knees. Rocket and I built stairs inside that lead to, believe it or not, a bookshelf. That's right, we made a book shelf made of books that held more books. It was pretty darn cool if I do say so myself.

This was a huge project that took us days; we worked on it all day Wednesday and into Thursday. I was actually kind of proud of it, it took a lot of thought but we did it. Rocket and I worked together well.

Once during construction, I laughed so hard the milk I was drinking came out of my nose.

We came up with projects for ourselves to pass the time while we were building our fort. For example, we would only put books with locations in the title at the entrances, so you would know you were going somewhere. Books like *Go North!* and *Women of the South* and *Train bound for China* and *West end School* were the archway around the doorframe.

The tunnels of our fort were lined with books that had some mystery in the name, such as *The Secret of the Mummy's Tomb* and *Buried Alive* and thankfully we found many Hardy Boys and Nancy Drew mysteries to fill the space.

The living areas were made with books about home life; *My little Puppy* and *Daddy's Home* were some examples.

Rocket wanted to do a room completely about animals and one about body functions (he's such a boy). It was difficult finding titles for that other than *Everybody Poops* and *The Gas We Pass*. It cracked him up.

Rocket and I were together a lot each day, but there were times I just sat and read in the library and he'd be off doing what ever it is he does. For the most part, I would end up fixing something he was trying to do or rescuing his butt from places like the rafters on the gym ceiling. I guess that's why I was so surprised on this particular morning. As I sat in our book fort reading, Rocket came in and asked if he could show me something.

"Sure" I said and followed him down the hall.

He lead me down the math hallway and by the language rooms to the back part of the school, not quite as far as the gym or the cafeteria. On the left, there was a door that was always shut, behind it were a set of stairs.

I don't want to say I didn't know they existed, I suppose I did, but I had never been down those stairs. I guess I knew they led to the trade shops, woodworking, metals, engine repair, but I hadn't had to take any of those classes yet.

The way our school schedule was set up was so that each seventh and eighth grade student took one year of home economics and then a year of a trade. The students could pick one trade, or you could pick what the school called "half trade" which meant that you got to pick two trades and take one class for half of the year and the other class after winter break. So, you might take woodworking and then engine repair, or metals and drafting, or you could take the full year in one class, it was up to the individual student.

However, everybody had to take a full year of home economics. We were learning how to cook, balance check books, balance home life and work and how to create a budget and live within what your projected income would be in the field you chose to work in. It was kind of like a years worth of reality outside of regular school work. The school wanted you to have some sense of what life was like after you graduate high school. It wasn't easy.

We even had to pick a weekend and carry around a sack of flour and care for it as if it was a baby. Both the boys and the girls had to do it. We had to pretend to feed it, dress it, rock it, and put it to bed. We even had to set our alarms to wake up during the night and pretend to feed it. After, we had to share our experiences with the class. I think most of the boys gave up by Saturday morning and a lot of the girls lied about getting up in the night. It was a tough assignment.

When I picked my weekend to carry the flour around, I carried it so much the bag wore down and flour started leaking everywhere. I broke my baby! I felt terrible. I didn't tell anybody, I taped it with bandaids but they stood out too much, so I removed them and put regular cellophane tape over the hole. It held for a while but by Sunday morning the bag was so week it broke apart. I was devastated! It was that moment that I decided I would never have children. I never told anyone what happened. I cleaned up the mess with broom, dust pan *and* vacuumed up my baby, and wrote my paper full of lies.

I followed Rocket down the stairs into this new world of classrooms. I was asking questions about each room I passed, but Rocket, as usual, wasn't answering. We came to the last room on the left and walked in.

"Whatdaya think?"

I shook my head in approval. It was a nice room. *Was*

that what he was asking me? There were lots of machines in there, I wasn't sure exactly what they did, but they sure looked important. So, I continued nodding. "Looks good." I affirmed.

"Come on, I'll show you around." Even though the room hadn't been used in almost a week, it smelled strongly of wood and saw dust and even though it looked as if it had been swept and cared for, there was still a layer a fine dust that covered everything.

Beyond the smell of wood was a faint smell that didn't belong there. I couldn't place it exactly, paint maybe. It distracted from the clean wood smell.

"So this is the belt sander', Rocket tapped a large machine in the corner, "and this little guy is the dovetailer."

I could tell he had a personal connection to that one.

"This right here, this is big Bertha." He rubbed his hand along a large machine. "This is where it all starts."

"What's it do?" I asked.

"She." Rocket corrected "What's *she* do? She is the most kick butt table saw in the world. This baby rips through wood like butter. This is where all of our projects start."

"Cool" I said. I was starting to feel nervous about next year. Maybe I'll just take drafting, I thought. I wasn't a big fan of computers, but I found Big Bertha slightly intimidating.

Then he took me to the back part of the classroom. At one point I referred to the room as a class room, but Rocket corrected me again.

"It's a shop" he said.

So, he took me to the back part of the shop into another smaller room. Shop? Room? I wasn't sure what this one was called. A smaller room.

There were all kinds of unfinished projects lying propped up on tables and benches and leaning against the walls. We walked slowly by each one. They were pretty good for a bunch of seventh or eighth graders. There were tables and book cases, coat racks and wooden boxes, all in different stages of being finished.

Rocket took a step back and let me pass him to examine each project myself. "These are pretty good." I said and turned to look at Rocket. He was just nodding his head slightly, he didn't say a word.

"Oooohhh, what's this one going to be?" I walked over and gently ran my hand down the side of the wood.

"That's Brice's chair. He's making a chair. See his use of the shaper on this part? He's really pretty talented."

"Ill say" I agreed.

Another piece caught my eye; "Oh my God Rocket! Look at this one!"

In the back of the room stood the most amazing cabinet I've even seen.

"It's an armoire."

"What's an armoire?" I asked, I couldn't take my eyes off of it.

"Its French. It's a cabinet for clothes." He opened the doors to show me the inside. "It was originally used for storing weapons, but I guess the women won out and started using them for their dresses and stuff."

I couldn't look away. It was just beautiful.

"It's almost done. Do you like it?"

"Like it? Rocket, its amazing! Who's is it? Is this the teacher's example piece?"

"It's mine." he interrupted my line of questioning. He spoke as if he was both proud and a little embarrassed.

"What?" I snapped my head around. "Rocket, this is store bought!"

He laughed a little. "Nope, I hung the doors this morning. I've been working on it all year."

"Can I touch it?"

"Go ahead." I ran my hands slowly around each smooth corner.

He had sanded the wood so cleanly, it almost looked plastic. It felt so good under my fingers, I couldn't take my hands off it. I think I was slowly falling in love with an armoire.

The drawers on the bottom slid in and out as if they moved themselves, the doors were thick and solid. The scroll work on the top was so intricate, I could not believe it was done by human hands. The feet holding the unit up were huge, like elephant feel, but just beautiful, they matched the scrollwork on the top. I rested my cheek against it. It was amazing.

"I have no words Rocket." I'm embarrassed to say, my eyes welled up a little. This thing was *that* good. I blinked quick so he didn't see the tears.

"Here, let me show you." I was glad he started talking. "See inside the drawers, see those little notches? Those are done on the dovetailer. See the drawer slides? Self-closing, see?"

He slid open a drawer and then shut it to about two inches of still being open and the drawer silently slid itself shut. He gave me a tour of the armoire.

I was still speechless. After a few minutes, I asked "What are you going to do with it?"

"Don't know." he shrugged. He answered so casually. I was surprised. A gorgeous work of art like this, surly he had something in mind for it, but he genuinely seemed like he didn't know.

"Are you going to bring it home? Give it to your Mom? You going to sell it?" I had a million questions as usual.

"I really don't know." he wasn't kidding.

I'm not sure exactly what it was about this experience and finding out about Rocket's talent that made me feel a little closer to him, but I did. Maybe its just that I'd spent so many years bailing him out of his 'brilliant ideas' and rescuing him from being an idiot that I never got to see this part of him. Today, I saw a little glimpse of Rocket, the man, the man he was becoming, the man he was going to be. It was nice.

Chapter 21

The Discovery

I stayed behind in the shop for a while and James stayed and watched me work. I had been there most of the morning and was pretty much done for the day, I just re-sanded some corners by hand and cleaned up.

We went upstairs and made lunch, James was catching on pretty quick in the kitchen, I had shared with her everything I knew about cooking. We worked well together.

After we had cleaned up we decided to go for a walk. We started on the ground floor and covered each hallway. As we walked we glanced into each classroom. We noticed that the signs we had hung on the first night here had begun to fall, the tape was peeling away. We also noticed it was blocking the sun and making the rooms dark when the lights weren't turned on. So, we stopped in each room and removed the signs. We crumpled each one as we went. By the time we reached the south hallway, we had a ball of paper so huge, we decided to play a little hallway volleyball with it.

We smashed it back and forth to each other down the hall. James threw it at me and I grabbed it and quickly changed the game. I ran with it down the hall like it was a football, I tried to tuck it in my arms as best I could, it was so big. I ran with one hand in front to block anyone from the tackle. I got to the end of the hallway and spiked it in the end zone. That was it for the ball. It fell to pieces. I gathered up the papers and stuffed them into a can in one of the class rooms.

The school sure had changed in my eyes over the last several days. Besides the messes we were leaving here and there, trash in trash cans, dishes in the sink in the kitchen, books all over the hallway, tools by the door with no handle, it had changed. Softened somehow.

Lately it seemed, not quiet like home, more like, I guess, camp. Yes, I thought to myself, it was like being at camp. Though I had never been to camp before, this was what I thought it must be like. A home away from home.

James went to camp every summer. Since we were little she was gone for two weeks every July to the same camp. I don't remember the name of it, and even though I hung out with Bill and Evan sometimes, I was always glad when she came back. We liked the same stupid stuff. James wasn't like a real girl, she was cool.

We skateboarded everywhere, or took our bikes. We weren't that close to the beach, but now that we were getting older, I suspected her parents would let us go alone this summer. We had gone alone twice before without telling anyone, but James felt too guilty and we left pretty quick. She was a good swimmer too and wasn't afraid of the rope swing. She could climb a tree like no one I have ever seen, and even though she couldn't cook, she made the best lemonade I've ever had. Her parents were pretty cool too. They had me over for dinner a lot and took me places. Even places I didn't want to go.

One time her mom needed to go shopping for a dress to wear to a wedding, or a funeral, or something, I wasn't paying much attention, and she made James come with her, and James made me go too. It was horrible. I hate shopping, but then, so does James, so we were miserable together. We did have some laughs though, it was okay.

We continued our walk through the school and decided instead of walking the hallway, we would walk through each classroom, just for something different. Each room was connected by a doorway, I'm not sure why. We thought it would be a little less boring to take that route. We started in the corner of the school. James walked as close as she could to the windows, I stood on the first desk and walked across the tops of the last row of desks, at the end, I'd hop down and enter the next classroom. At the rear south corner, there were two classrooms that left their hallway doors locked, but we were still able to access them from the adjoining room. During my hunt for vending machine money, I never went into these rooms. I had been entering each room from the hallway and when I found these doors locked, I had just moved on.

We went in and I immediately went to rummage through the teachers desk, I found only a penny.

"Rocket, really? Give it up." James was not thrilled with the idea of my rummaging.

We entered the final classroom on that south hallway. I ran to the front of the room to the teachers desk, James was walking the perimeter. When she came to the corner, she stopped short.

"Rocket?" she sounded cautious in her tone. "Rocket, what's that?"

I looked up from the desk. "What's what?" I had no idea what she was talking about.

"That" she pointed, but I was elbow deep in the top drawer and couldn't see.

"I dunno."

"Rocket! For the love of Pete, would you please stop fishing for money and look!"

I looked up. She was pointing to a ladder. It was metal and

screwed to the wall, its bottom rung was about 5 feet off the ground, it had been painted the same color as the wall and the metal bars that it was made of were so thin, it was barely noticeable.

"It's a ladder." I said "so what?"

"Rocket, look." She pointed up. There was a square panel cut into the ceiling. "Where do you think it leads to?"

She had my interest. I got up and walked over. "Looks like maybe an attic? I don't know. Quick! Bring that desk over."

We slid the desk under the ladder and I started to climb. It wasn't much of a climb, just a few rungs and I could reach the panel. I started to push but it didn't budge. It was obvious it had been painted over a few times and the paint had sealed it in place. I pushed harder. It wasn't moving. "James, run to the janitors closet and find something I can use to pry this open! Quick!"

James ran. I jumped down. I stayed behind and looked around the room for anything that might help. I grabbed a hard cover book and climbed back up. I started smashing the book into the panel. Nothing. I jumped down again. I remembered in my rummaging that there was a ruler in the teachers desk, I ran and got it. I climbed back up and tried shoving the ruler under the edges that were painted shut, but the ruler broke after three tries. I hung from the ladder and tried to get my foot high enough to kick at it and got nowhere. When James returned she was breathless from running, she had with her a hammer, a flathead screwdriver, a putty knife and some potato chips.

"Where'd you get the chips?"

"I had a craving for them, so I swung by the caf on the way back." I loved how she thought sometimes.

She offered me the bag, I smashed a bunch in my mouth, took the hammer and the putty knife and climbed back up. That was it. That was exactly what we needed. The panel began to come loose. I kept hammering. James was bouncing up and down below me.

"Come on Rocket." I heard her whisper. She was squinting as she looked up at the work I was doing. The more I hammered, the more paint chips rained down on her and she had to move. Finally, it broke loose! I slid the panel to the side inside of the ceiling.

"YEA!" James yelled.

"Yea," I agreed, "just one thing, how do we get up there?" The wall ladder went to the ceiling but it was only inches from the wall and didn't give any angle to get up into the ceiling. I gave my best effort.

"Move the desk in case I fall." I instructed James. She did. I positioned my feet as close to the rung my hand was on as I could and sort of leaned and sprung at the same time. I missed. I came crashing to the floor, but landed on my feet somehow. We slid the desk back over and up I went again. I did the same thing with the same result, only this time I didn't land on my feet. James cracked up. She always laughed when I hurt myself.

"Glad I could be so entertaining." I said sarcastically.

"Sorry." she said and regained composure. Up I went again. I tried to angle myself differently this time but had no luck. I just couldn't get enough leverage to pull myself through the hole.

Chapter 22

The Escape Hatch

"Why don't you let me try?" watching Rocket was certainly entertaining, but we weren't getting anywhere. My body was smaller and lighter and I had been known to be a decent tree climber, so I sort of pushed him out of the way as he went to get back on top of the desk again.

I beat him to the first rung and hoisted myself up the ladder. At the top, I reached out and grabbed the edge of where the panel had been, I counted to three and thrust my left arm out to grab hold. I did it. I made it on the first try! I pulled myself up and through the hole in the ceiling into the darkness above. I was excited and nervous all at the same time. I found myself up in a tiny crawlspace above the world below.

"What's up there?" Rocket yelled up to me.

I hung my head through the hole. "Don't know yet, hold on."

"You look like an octopus!"

"What?"

"All your hair is hanging down like tenticles! You look like an octopus!" Rocket laughed. I rolled my eyes.

"I'm going exploring."

"What's up there? he yelled again.

"Hang on", I yelled back "I have to spin my body around and there's no space to do it up here." I spun on my belly in the foot of space I had above me. I saw it as soon as I turned around. "Rocket! I see light!"

"Like, light, or like *sunlight*."

"Sunlight I think!"

"What is it? What do you see? Can we get out?" this time it was Rocket with all the questions.

Chapter 23

Getting Out

I was dying with curiosity and she was giving me nothing. No answer. I couldn't wait! Then I heard a very distant "WHOOOO HOOOOO!" and footsteps above me.

"Rocket! I'm on the roof! The roof, Rocket! Get up here now!" James yelled. "Its beautiful! The most beautiful roof I've ever seen!"

I looked frantically around the room trying to find anything that could get me up high enough to get myself through the hole. I pushed a desk underneath and found a metal chair in the corner and put it on the desk. I climbed on top of both but only got close enough to get my head through. I peeked up and saw the hatch to the roof and the sun shining through.

I jumped back down to find something to get me closer and up higher. I spotted a book shelf. I ran and grabbed 5 hardcovers and put them on top of the chair, but because of the angle of the chair they all slid off.

The ruler I had broken earlier was on the floor, I grabbed the biggest piece and decided it would make a good brace to fasten the books together. I needed duct tape. I looked up into the hole and yelled to James that I would be right back. I raced to the janitors closet on the first floor.

I ran fast when the car was outside the door on our first day of this lock-in and thought I ran even faster when our principal was in the building, but this time, well, I don't think I've ever run so fast in my entire life.

We had built our book fort right between where I was standing and the janitors closet. I didn't have the heart to knock it down to get by, so I got down on my knees and crawled through. This was taking too much time! I got up and out of the fort and started running again.

I almost ran right by the door. As I skidded to a stop, I flung the door open, spotted the duct tape, grabbed it and ran. I ran in the opposite direction so I didn't have to belly crawl through books again. Up the stairs three at a time, I ran down the hall and back to the room. The room of freedom.

I lined the books up, placed the ruler on the side and wrapped the whole thing in a duct tape bundle and threw it back up on the chair.

I climbed up onto the desk, and then up onto the pile of books on top of the chair.

That was better, I was through the hole up to my shoulders. I reached my arms through and with all my strength, started to pull myself up. I got my right side up and tried to straighten my left elbow but it buckled under me and I went crashing down on top of everything under me. I laid on the floor for a moment surveying my injuries.

I had too much adrenaline rushing through me to feel hurt, I was too excited. I got up slowly and repositioned everything, desk, chair, books. I climbed up again.

In the distance I could hear James yelling to me but she was way over on the other side of the building by now. I pulled myself through this time and wormed my way into the crawl space. Again, I was belly crawling and got myself to the hatch. I poked my head out and pulled my body through. I was out! It was amazing!

Chapter 24

Stuck Again

"Rocket! C'mere!" I yelled from the North West corner of the building. I couldn't believe how much I had missed the sunshine. The gentle breeze on my skin, the warmth of the sun, it all felt amazing.

In the first moments I was on the roof, I stood for a moment and took it all in. Then I began to walk the perimeter. I was trying desperately to find a way down; a way to get us free.

I looked over at Rocket. Even though he'd never say it, or even think it, I could tell he was enjoying being outside too. It was interesting what seven days of being indoors could do to a person. He was smiling.

As I walked around looking for a way down I found that there was nothing on any part of the building that I could see that we could climb down on. Even if we were the best rock climbers on earth, there was nothing to grab onto, or plant our feet on. The building was smooth all the way around.

I could see one window we had left open. It stuck out about 6 inches from the building, but even if we could get our feet on it, it would never hold our weight, the window would shut and we would be history.

We were stuck again, but at least we were outside.

Chapter 25

Hanging Out

"HELLO!" I yelled from the roof top. "HELLO! HELP! CAN ANYBODY HEAR ME? HELP US!" It was a useless attempt, I knew that, but I didn't know exactly what to do.

The road to the school was long and windy and trees lines the entire perimeter of the property, they would absorb the sound. Not only that, but the cross street at the top of where you turn into the road to the school was a main street and the sound of the traffic would drowned me out anyway. James laughed at my attempts.

"Its beautiful up here." she said and spun around with her arms outstretched.

Being cooped up weighed on us more than I had realized.

I laid down on the roof with my head hanging over the side, it was a neat feeling, scaring and exhilarating at the same time. The tar on the roof was warm from the sun, it felt nice under my belly.

James continued to walk around looking for a way down. After she exhausted her efforts, she came and laid next to me and hung her head over too.

"This is cool." she said. "Everything looks so peaceful from up here."

"Uh hu."

James rolled over onto her back and hung her head over the edge upside down. "Oh my God, Rocket, try this!"

I rolled. It was a little too freaky for me. I told her I was uncomfortable and rolled back. We laid there for a while listening to the sounds of the earth, the birds singing, the wind blowing through the leaves, the sound of distant traffic. I fell asleep. I woke to James kicking my feet.

"Rocket, here, take this. Rocket, wake up, take this." She was handing me something.

I was stiff from lying in this position and even though it was early evening, the sun was still bright in the sky, it was blinding after sleeping and I couldn't see what she was handing me.

"Here, I made hot dogs for dinner. Take yours."

Perfect idea. She had boiled us some hot dogs and wrapped them in bread. She knew I liked mine smothered in ketchup with only a dash of mustard and that's how she had prepared it.

"I thought it might be nice to have a picnic up here." James said.

It was. We ate in silence and watched the sun as it declined in the sky.

"Hey Rocket, remember the time I dragged you to go shopping with my mom?" James asked.

"Uh hu."

"Remember how you tried on that wet suit in the dressing room and it was way too small and you got stuck in it?"

"Uh hu." I smiled at the memory.

"We had to get a male employee to go in the dressing room and.." now James was cracking up. "And pull you out of it." She was laughing even harder now at the thought.

I started laughing too. "That actually hurt, getting extracted from that thing. It was so stuck to my body!" It was pretty funny.

"So what about the time," I countered, "we were swimming at the rope swing and you came out covered in leeches!"

"That was disgusting!" she laughed

"You were so freaked out, I had to pull them all off of you!"

"I know! I know!" she laughed and grimaced at the same time.

"You were dancing around and jumping and trying to shake them off of you. It looked like you were doing a Native American rain dance! I could barely get them off of you, you were squirming around so much!" We both laughed at my replicating her jumping and squirming.

"How about the time you bet I couldn't eat an entire slice of pizza in two bites. I rolled it up into a tight little pizza log and.."

"And you did it! That was really clever of you!"

"Except that I couldn't breath because my mouth was so full of pizza, you ended up having to pull some out of my mouth!"

"I know! That was disgusting too!"

We were both laughing so hard. Tears ran down James's cheeks.

"We've done a lot of kooky things." She held out her hand for a fist bump. "How about the guy...oh, what was his name... the guy at the storage locker auction your mom took us to... what did you call him again? Slimy Steve?"

"That's right! Slimy Steve in his tight leather pants and his hair slicked back with all that grease! We laughed about him forever!" We sat and talked about all the fun we've had together.

"And now this." I said.

"This?"

"Yeah, this."

"This what?"

"All of this." I said. "I know it stinks we missed April vacation, but I've actually had a good time this week."

"Yeah," she said wistfully. "I guess it has been an adventure.

And having dinner up here on the roof is nice." She thought for a second. "I guess I would classify this as one of our fun times. Certainly a story to share with our children."

"I know, right?"

"They'll never believe us."

"I know, right?"

"I'll say to them, there was a time when I was young, I think it was seventh grade, when me and my best friend Rocket got locked inside the school for a whole week! And do you know what my kids will say?"

"What?"

"They'll say 'You had a friend named Rocket?'" and they'll laugh.

"Shut up James" I said quietly and leaned into her. "That whole rocket idea was a good one, it should have worked."

"Rocket, we were seven."

"Yeah, I guess." I shrugged. We sat quietly for a long time enjoying the night. The sun had gone down and the air was cool but still humid. The bugs had started to come out, but they were bearable.

"James?" I said and broke the silence.

"Yeah?"

"Do you think your mom and dad can get that armoire into their truck?"

"Sure, I don't see why not."

"I've decided what I want to do with it."

James shifted her position, she was paying attention. "What?"

"I want you to have it."

"What? Rocket..." she started to say something.

I was hoping she wasn't going to get all mushy on me. She didn't. James is good like that.

"Rocket, what about your mom? Wouldn't she want it."

"Probably, but I'm afraid she'd try to sell it or something. Plus, it goes good with your furniture."

"I don't know what to say, David, that's really nice. Really nice."

"James?"

"Yeah?"

"Don't ever call me David again."

"Okay" we both laughed together.

James stood up and started doing a kooky little dance on the roof and singing "Rock-et Rock-et Rocket Rocket." over and over.

"I'm heading in," she said and we both climbed down through the hatch, back into our school.

Chapter 26

Boarding the Roof

Friday dawned sunny and humid. The roof was almost unbearable, the sun beat down and the moisture content in the air made it hard to even move. Rocket and I still spent as much time as we could up on the roof, it sure beat being stuck inside.

Rocket brought his skateboard up there, which I insisted was a stupid idea, but, once he gets an idea in his head, its pretty hard to tell him otherwise. He said it was a nice flat space to ride and the vent pipes made cool obstacles to go around. He was careful to stay far away from the edges.

We could only stay outside for about a half hour at a time, sometimes we had to go in and just lie on our backs on the cool tile floor of the classrooms. We didn't move around too much on Friday, it was just too hot.

We had three days left to get through before Monday would come and school would be in session again and we would be let out.

Silly as it sounds, I had a little problem with that, you see, I had a perfect attendance record so far this year.

When Monday came, I would have to go home. Mom and

Dad were due back Sunday afternoon, they were planning on dropping off all of their suitcases at home, and then coming to get me at Nanny's. I'm sure they would be frantic if I wasn't there. Police would be called, I really *had* to go home. But what about my attendance record? I didn't want to mess that up either. I guess I could call them from school if the phones were fixed by then. Another problem was I had been wearing the same clothes all week, I needed a shower, and a hairbrush.

Rocket made a sort of nacho plate for lunch, potato chips, melted cheese, chopped tomatoes and onions, it was a perfect lunch for such a hot day. We had chopped fruit and made our own whipped cream for dessert. After lunch we went back to the roof. I sat in the sun and watched Rocket maneuver his skateboard around the vent pipes, enjoying the breezes he created while riding.

He tried several paths and routes he created over and over again. I was just too hot. I sat watching him most of the time. Sometimes I would walk around trying to create a breeze just by walking. I boarded a couple of times too, but was too nervous having a skateboard on the roof.

I sat with my feet dangling over the edge of the building and watched the cumulonimbus clouds build thunderheads on the horizon. I was hoping for a huge rain storm to break the humidity, and lightening always seemed to clear the air of any negativity and the rain would have cooled the horribly hot day.

"I wish it would rain," I said.

"I know" Rocket answered back breathlessly. He jumped off his board and came to join me on the edge. He kicked his board forward to move it closer to me, but he used too much force. The skateboard went sailing over the edge of the roof into a bush below. I cupped my hands to my mouth as I watched it go over.

"Oh my God, Rocket," I laughed.

"Oh my God" he said back and looked below in disbelief.

"OK" I clapped my hands together and swung my legs up to stand. "So, that's that. Now what would you like to do?"

We were both smiling, but Rocket was still looking at the bushes below and shaking his head.

"How 'bout some hoops? Wanna go play inside?"

"I guess so." Rocket answered "Too darn hot out here anyway." He stood up and we walked over to the hatch together.

"Better close that incase it rains." I said, Rocket agreed.

Inside, we were careful to close not only the hatch to the roof, but we slid the ceiling panel over as well.

The top floor of the school was pretty warm, so we planned on heading right for the gym, it was on the ground floor and had a concrete floor and walls and was generally pretty cool.

We passed the caf on the way and decided to stop and grab a cold drink. Milk just didn't seem to be what we needed on such a hot day, so we dug around and found some fake lemon juice, we added it to water and poured in a bunch of sugar. The sugar wouldn't melt in the water, so it wasn't exactly the best lemonade, but it was cold and we chugged it down. Then we headed for the gym.

Chapter 27

More Rain's Coming

It was very much in the forefront of my mind that today was Friday, three more days and I could go home. Its true I enjoyed my week with James, but I was craving a hot shower (I think that is the very first time I ever thought that, usually bathing didn't cross my mind much) and I was just bored of the school. Although, I have to admit, school certainly did not feel like school anymore. It wasn't a place of learning, it was a place of living. The science lab felt like *my* science lab, the kitchen felt like mine as well. I was sure James felt the same about the library since she started sleeping in there.

We played a couple games of 21 in the gym, being certain to put away the basketball in the exact place we found it. I suggested to James that we make a campfire on the roof and maybe it would attract attention and we would be rescued. She was pretty quick to point out what a dumb idea that was. Whatever. I guess she was right.

I made a simple dinner of tuna salad sandwiches, since the day had been so hot, I didn't want to turn on the oven, or even eat hot food for that matter. We took our sandwiches up to the roof, it had very quickly become our favorite place. It was late in the day and it had started to cool a bit, though it was still very humid. We ate our sandwiches and just sat. That was one of the nice things about my relationship with James, we could just sit and be quiet, we didn't have to be talking all the time. Silence was not uncomfortable.

We watched the sun go down without much comment. The rain clouds were still on the horizon and were not yet a threat to us. We lay on our backs and watched the stars, what we could see of them through the hazy night sky.

We talked a little about our release on Monday. James was worried about her attendance record, I just wanted to go home. I missed television, my room, a toothbrush. Plus, I still felt like the school owed us a vacation anyway. I mean really, if you spend your vacation at the one place you are supposed to be away from, you should get a bonus week off. Sounded perfectly logical to me. James only partially agreed.

Chapter 28

The Ladder

As we lay on the roof watching the stars, I was swarmed by mosquitoes. Apparently, I am bug repellent for other people. Rocket lay still as the blood suckers flew right past him and found what they were looking for on my face, neck and in my ears. Their high pitched humming was driving me insane. Still, it was nice laying there, even with my constant flailing. I looked like I was riding a bicycle upside down with my legs turning the peddles in the air and my arms swatting at my face.

Rocket and I had had an interesting week and the feeling that the end of this craziness was close to over was real. Lying here on the roof was a nice close to a strange week.

It was hard to imagine that leaving this place was even more complicated than being here in the first place. There would be a lot of people that would want to talk to us, parents, teachers, the principal. It was all pretty overwhelming, so I continued to try and appreciate where I was at that moment. I guess I never realized it before, but being with Rocket made me feel safe. I was okay here and now.

I noticed Rocket swat at a bug, and then another until I

realized what he thought were bugs were rain drops. The rain had begun. On instinct, we both stood to go inside.

"Wait, Rocket?" he looked at me in the darkness. "Lets stay out here in the rain."

Rocket shrugged. "Cool" he said and we moved over to the ledge to sit and dangle our feet over and watch the rain clouds move ominously toward us.

In the distance we could hear thunder. There were flashes of lightening too but they were pretty far away. We sat for a moment and let the rain shoo away the bugs, and begin to trickle down our faces. One of those rain drops, the big fat ones that land in the middle of your scalp and feel so weird fell on my head. It felt like someone slapped me and I ducked. Rocket got a big laugh out of that one. Suddenly the sky opened up and within a moment, we were drenched. There were puddles on the roof and we danced and splashed in them and tried to get each other even wetter than we already were, if that was even possible. Thunder crashed right above our head and we both jumped, and then froze, and then ran to the hatch and climbed in as fast as we could.

We had left the hatch open when we came out and a puddle was forming inside the ceiling, we let ourselves drop to the floor (we were getting good at getting in and out) and then went to find paper towels to clean the rain puddle up.

We closed up the ceiling panel and went to find a bedtime snack in the cafeteria. The storm outside raged, thunder was right over the building and the lightening was almost nonstop.

We both decided to spend the night in the library, it had the most windows and we could watch the lightening as we drifted off to sleep. I didn't say anything to Rocket, but I think it wasn't so much the lightening show he wanted to see, as it was he wanted my company during the storm. I slept on the couch, Rocket was on the floor right beside me.

I'm not sure what time it was, but during the night we were awakened by the loudest crash I've ever heard.

We both sat straight up and simultaneously said "What was that?" I was shaking so bad, I couldn't get up.

"You really should go check and see what that was." I instructed Rocket.

He wasn't nearly as concerned as I was, he had already rolled back over.

"Rocket!" I yelled. It sounded like a truck drove through the school.

"What?" he said sleepily.

"Go see what that was!"

"Why don't *you* go see."

"Let's go together."

"James, can't this wait until morning?" I didn't have an answer for that. I wanted an answer to my own question, I wanted to know what the noise was, but I wanted to have Rocket check it out, or at least be more awake if we went together.

He was already back to sleep. I stayed sitting up for a while longer. I listened carefully to the silence around me. I could hear the rain pounding outside, the thunder continued but it seemed like it was getting farther away. I could still see flashes of lightening too. I drifted off a couple of times, but woke up to listen again and again. It was a tough night.

The morning brought the nicest day. The humidity was gone and the air was cool. There were barely any clouds in the sky, I was dying to get up on the roof and enjoy the day.

Rocket woke and finally agreed to walk the school with me and check out what made the noise we heard. We walked each hall way and peeked in each room as we walked by. The school seemed in tact. I wished I knew the source of what crashed, but I guessed it didn't really matter anymore.

We made breakfast and talked about plans for the day. I really wanted to find a book and head up onto the roof and read in the sunshine. Since I had read so much this week, it was difficult finding another book to hold my interest and almost all of the library books were part of our fort. I looked around the fort and found *A Tall Tale* the story of tigers that were raised by humans. The only problem was it was on the bottom of the fort, holding up a wall. The fort took a lot of effort, but frankly, I was tired of it, so I grabbed the book and pulled. The wall came tumbling down. I felt bad for tearing it down, so I stacked the pile of books up as neatly as I could.

I wasn't sure where Rocket was, but I had my book and my plans for the day and headed to the roof. I slid the ceiling panel away and belly crawled to the hatch. I flung that open and hoisted my body up, this was becoming very familiar and easy to do.

Once I was standing on the roof, I surveyed the roof to find a comfortable spot to sit and read, as I turned to look behind me, I saw it. I could not believe what I was looking at! There it was, the answer to every question I had asked.

"ROCKET!" I screamed and went for the hatch. "ROCKET!" I screamed again. "ROCKET WHERE ARE YOU?" "ROCKET! GET OVER HERE! I NEED YOU NOW!"

I lowered myself down the hatch and then through the ceiling panel, I was moving so fast, I was shaking with excitement. I fell out of the ceiling. I twisted my ankle on landing but I didn't care.

"ROCKET!" I continued to scream. *Where was that boy?* I ran down the hall way hoping I wouldn't miss him should he come up the other side of the school.

"ROCKET!" I ran down the hall and turned the corner, I bumped straight into him.

"Whoa, what's going on?" he asked "What's the rush?"

I was breathless, I couldn't speak. I tried to talk and each word came out sounding more like whales talking. I made clicks and groans.

Finally, I was able to say "ROOF!" as I pointed.

"Very nice dog impression, J" Rocket laughed.

"Not...dog..." I said as I ran "Roof!" I pointed again and he followed.

We arrived at the classroom with the roof hatch, I guess I had knocked over several desks on my rush to find Rocket.

"What the heck happened here?"

"Not important, roof." My chest was heaving as I tried to breathe.

"Okay, okay, I'm going." He pulled himself through the hole, I went next.

"Hey!" Rocket said when he saw it. "That must have been what made the crashing sound last night!"

"Rocket!" I started pulling at my own hair. "Yes, that's right," I panted, "More though, Rocket, that's our way out of here!"

We both walked over to examine the tree that had fallen over onto the roof. It was leaning perfectly from the roof to the ground, it was tipped just the right way, it was our ladder down.

Chapter 29

James Wants to Wait

J ames and I got closer and examined the tree, we tried to push it, move it, shake it, we wanted to be certain it would support us as we climbed down, it seemed pretty secure. I started to climb on.

"Wait!" said James "Not yet."

"Whatdaya mean, not yet? James, we've been dying and trying to get out of here for a week. I'm gone baby, see ya later!" I swung my leg around the tip of the old pine tree, the part the star would have been placed should this have been a Christmas tree.

"Rocket, wait. It doesn't feel right to do it this way."

"What are you talking about?"

"Rocket, we've been missing for a week, if we leave now, and just walk down the street as if nothing ever happened, I'm afraid we'll be picked up by police or swarmed by reporters or something. I don't want that kind of attention. I just want to go home."

"James, don't you think if anyone even noticed we were gone, the police already would have looked for us here? My own mother probably hasn't been home much this week and your parents are across the Atlantic. Let's go."

"I just don't want to be seen walking away from here, can we at least wait until its dark out?" She was talking crazy. I was leaving now. I was hoping she would come with me, but if she didn't, so be it.

"Alright, alright," she agreed. "Just wait here one minute." and she took off. She ran back to the hatch and disappeared.

I started to size up the tree while I waited, I checked how each branch was situated and the level of difficulty it would be to get down.

James arrived shortly after with both of our back packs.

"OK I'm ready." she said and handed me my pack.

"Thanks." I said but I was really thinking; *Really James? You went back inside for this?*

I put my pack on and started down the tree. The numerous tiny branches at the top and all the pine needles made it more difficult than it seemed. I climbed back up onto the roof.

"Why don't you go first?" I asked James. "Go ahead, I'll follow."

She kind of snickered, I'm not sure why, but with a smile, she grabbed on to the tree. I watched her footing closely and tried to copy her. She really was good at this. She scaled each branch like she was part monkey. She was going too fast.

"Wait up!" I called with a face full of pine needles.

"Come on!" she called back.

I was trying to look down and behind me to mimic her footing and that's when I slipped. The weight of my back pack pulled me over and soon I was hanging 30 feet in the air with my back to the ground. I wrapped my legs even tighter around the trunk, thankfully we were still up high enough and the trunk was thin. James must have heard the rustle of the branches and she climbed back up to where I was and pulled at my jeans to twist me back over.

I found the leverage I needed and pulled myself back. We continued climbing down over the thick branches, ducking under others. It was an obstacle course of bark and needles and twigs and branches. We arrived near the bottom and found there to be no branches, only trunk, we would have to shimmy our way to the ground.

Chapter 30

Say Hello to Sara

I was the first to hop out of the tree. I had only minor injuries, some scratches on my arms. My hands were black with sap and dirt and my head was full of pine needles. I gave my head a shake and it snowed green.

Rocket hopped out a few seconds later, he did the same. We stood there looking at each other. It was strange. Like our first day locked in the school, we really didn't know what to do next. Without a word, we turned and started to walk away from the school, our school.

"Oh, hold on a sec!" and Rocket started to run back to the school.

I waited.

He fished around in the bushes and grabbed his skateboard and we started down the long winding road. We didn't speak a word. About 30 yards from the school I heard a noise, a rustling in the trees to my left. It caught my attention and I looked over. There was a bird on the lowest branch flapping its wings. I stopped.

"Rocket." I held his arm to stop him from walking. I jutted my chin toward the tree. "Its Sara." I said and felt a little nostalgic.

"Hey cool. S'up Max." he said and we continued on.

The world seemed so different, changed, quieter, softer. Cars whizzed by us on the main road and nobody even looked at us, I tried not to make eye contact with the drivers. I'm not sure why.

Rocket and I didn't say a word the whole walk home.

When we arrived at the corner where he would continue straight toward the park and I would turn right, we stopped not knowing what to say.

Rocket broke the silence. "So, ah, I guess I'll see you on Monday hu?"

"Guess so." I answered.

"See ya."

"Bye." I stood for a minute and watched him walk away. Once he looked back and gave a little wave. "Bye" I whispered.

When I arrived at home, it felt cold, empty, un-lived in. "Hello!" I yelled knowing full well that no one was there.

I walked into the kitchen and opened the fridge, empty. Mom had made sure we used up everything before they left. I looked in the cabinets, there was not much choice. I decided to shower first.

It was the best shower of my life, I even brought my toothbrush into the shower with me and brushed for what felt like a half an hour. I let the warm water just run over me, I've never felt so clean in my entire life.

After, I dressed and went to the kitchen, I made tuna salad and then realized there was no bread. I dished a couple of fork fulls into my mouth, but without bread, I really didn't want it, so I dumped it in the sink, rinsed out my bowl and walked into Mom and Dad's room.

Now, I knew that Dad kept what he called "emergency money" in his top drawer. I also knew that I was never to touch it. I really didn't know what to do. I closed my eyes and grabbed the money and went back to the kitchen to call a cab.

Chapter 31

The Cereal Fooled My Mom

I walked up the path to my front door and my mother whipped it open before I could reach for the door knob. "Where have you been?" she said, she sounded angry.

I opened my mouth to answer and before I could, I saw her looking at my back pack, I thought she would piece the whole story together in her head, but she didn't.

"Oh, were you over James's doing homework?"

"Something like that." I said. I saw her soften.

I squeezed by her into the apartment and she followed.

"I need to talk to you about something."

"Yeah?" I felt exhausted.

"Once again you have eaten every bit of cereal in this house, I really need to you remember you live with other people. I know you're a growing boy, but really, the whole box in one day? I'm not going to be able to afford to feed you anymore."

I stood looking at her blankly. She tosseled my hair and pulled out a pine needle.

"Just go easy, OK?" and she walked away.

Her husband Mark was a cereal fiend. He constantly ate

every box and left the empties in the cupboard. Mom always blamed me. He was never around to take the heat, so I would just shrug. Whatever. She never even noticed I was gone. I was glad. I didn't have the energy to explain the whole story. I dropped my pack and headed right for the shower.

Chapter 32

Back to Normal?

The cab pulled up in front of Nanny's house just as her nurse was leaving. She gave me a polite wave as she got into her car. The nurse didn't speak much English, if any at all and I was glad, I didn't feel much like talking.

Inside, I saw my packed suitcases leaning against the living room wall, on top was my cell phone, completely dead of course. I pulled the charger out of the front pocket of the suitcase and plugged it in.

I walked into the room off of the living room where Nanny's bed was. She was there. She smiled when she saw me and then began yelling at me, well, not yelling at *me*, she kept calling me Nancy. I let her yell and walked over and kissed her forehead.

I busied myself around her house, I dusted and cleaned and picked up some newspapers left by the nurse.

I made something to eat and sat in the living room by my suitcases. When my phone had a little life to it, I saw there were 15 messages. I listened as my mom went on and on about their trip and what she had seen each day. At the end of each message she would instruct me not to call her back as she kept her phone shut off during the day. She said she was sorry she kept missing me. I snickered and shook my head.

Mom and Dad arrived on Sunday right on schedule to pick me up. There were big hugs and kisses all around. I was happy to see them, but felt changed somehow, different, grown up. They asked about my week and I just shrugged and said it was fine. They visited with Nanny for a bit but said they were eager to get home, and we left.

Chapter 33

Back to School

Monday arrived and the school was all abuzz. First, there was a tree leaning on the roof and was causing quiet a stir. There were teachers positioned around it so that no one would try to climb it.

Next, students and faculty were trying desperately to figure out who broke into the school, built a fort of books and left. The librarian stood over a pile of books in the hallway shaking her head. I went straight to home room.

Ms Bethany was tanned and relaxed and she looked very happy.

Our first class was reading.

"While I choose our next book for the semester, I would like you all to take out your notebooks. I want a detailed essay on how you spent your April vacation."

I looked at the blank notebook paper on my desk. I glanced around the room at everybody writing a million miles an hour. I looked back at my blank page, smiled and began to write the title of my essay. "MY WEEK AT THE BEACH."

CPSIA information can be obtained at www.ICGtesting.com
Printed in the USA
BVOW08s1742131015

422245BV00001B/2/P